In Want of a Wife

A Pride and Prejudice Vagary

by

Regina Jeffers

Regency Solutions

Copyright ©2019 by Regina Jeffers
Cover and Interior Text Design by Sarah Callaham with SKC Design
Cover Image via Victoria Cooper Art
All Rights Reserved

This is a work of fiction. Names, places, characters and incidents are either the product of the author's imagination or are used fictitiously, and any resemblance to any actual persons, living or dead, businesses, organizations, events or locales is entirely coincidental. All trademarks, service marks, registered trademarks, and registered service marks are the property of their respective owners and are used herein for identification purposes only. The publisher does not have any control over or assume any responsibility for author or third-party websites or their contents.

All rights Reserved under International and Pan-American Copyright Conventions. No part of this book may be used or reproduced, transmitted, downloaded, decompiled, reverse engineered, or stored in or introduced into any information storage and retrieval system, in any form or by any means whether electronic or mechanical, including photocopying, recording, etc., now known or hereinafter invented without the written permission from the author and copyright owner except in the case of brief quotation embodied in critical articles and reviews.

WARNING: The unauthorized reproduction or distribution of this copyrighted work is illegal. Criminal copyright infringement, including infringement without monetary gain, is investigated by the FBI and is punishable by up to 5 years in federal prison and a fine of $250,000. Anyone pirating ebooks will be prosecuted to the fullest extent of the law and may be liable for each individual download resulting there from.

ABOUT THE PRINT VERSION: If you purchased a print version of this book without a cover, you should be aware that the book is stolen property. It was reported as "unsold and destroyed" to the publisher, and neither the author nor the publisher has received any payment for this "stripped book."

IF YOU FIND AN EBOOK OR PRINT VERSION OF THIS BOOK BEING SOLD OR SHARED ILLEGALLY, PLEASE REPORT IT. By payment of required fees, the purchaser has been granted the *non*-exclusive, *non*-transferable right to access and read the text of this eBook. The reverse engineering, uploading, and/or distributing of this eBook via the internet or via any other means without the permission of the copyright owner is illegal and punishable by law. Please purchase only authorized electronic editions and do not participate in or encourage electronic piracy of copyrighted materials. Your support of the author's rights is appreciated.

In Want of a Wife

A Pride and Prejudice Vagary

Regina Jeffers

Regency Solutions

Chapter 1

"OPEN YOUR EYES, ELIZABETH," a voice near her ear demanded, but she could not seem to find the strength to lift her lids. A pain so intense that the idea of her willingly encountering it caused her to grimace.

"Come, love," the same voice insisted. It was a very nice voice. Smooth baritone. Cultured. A slight accent buried within the words.

Even so, a hint of fear skittered up her spine. She attempted to shake off the idea, but pain — immediate and excruciating — had her squeezing her eyes even tighter. Instinctively, she reached for her head, but he stopped her, catching her hand in his, bringing it to his lips. The warmth of his breath across her knuckles was comforting in an odd sort of manner; yet, she knew she should not be permitting him to continue to caress her fingers. She gave a little tug, but he enclosed her hand in his two.

"Easy," he cautioned. "You have injured your head. My personal physician has treated the laceration and applied a bandage. Just know, you are safe now. I will protect you. Nothing and no one will harm you again."

Despite his assurances, she did not feel safe. Instead, foreboding crept into her chest, constricting her breathing. She attempted to remember what had happened to her, but she could recall nothing of the details. Questions. What felt to be hundreds of them scampered through her mind, but none she could name, except one. She cracked one eyelid open and then the second, attempting to focus upon his features. Forcing moisture to her lips, she rasped, "Who are you?"

The effort exhausted her, and her eyes drifted closed again.

"Surely you know me," he protested. His words sounded as if he held his emotions tightly in check. "I am William. Your husband."

She thought to protest, but the darkness had caught her other hand and was leading her away from him. With one final attempt to correct his declaration, her mind formed the words, but her lips would not cooperate. Her dissent died before she could tell him: *I do not have a husband!*

The next time she woke, she was alone in what appeared to be a finely furnished room. Even without turning her head, she could view the yellow and green flounce on the bed drape and the bright sunlight shining through the window. Tentatively, her hand reached for what felt to be a bandage wrapped about her forehead. As the man had told her previously, she had been injured. But how? When? Why? Another shooting pain crossed behind her eyes, and she winced, squeezing her eyes shut.

Seeking a calming breath, she attempted to remember how she had come to this place. Slowly, she lowered her hand and opened her eyes. A memory flitted closer: A voice called to her in urgency. *Elizabeth! Lizzy!* And the same voice saying: *I am William. Your husband.*

The idea frightened her, for she knew, without a doubt, she could have no husband. Her father would never. . . . Her father? *Who was her father?* She glanced to her hand where a very prominent emerald ring rested on her finger. "That is not right," she whispered in labored syllables. Yet, as her lips formed the words, another memory — this one of fire rising up and consuming everything, and then of the sun, so sharp it stung her eyes — raced across her mind. A strong hand held hers. A man's hand. A gold band bearing a signet upon his finger. His hand soothing hers and his voice — the same voice as the stranger — pleading with her to stay with him.

She knew instantly she did not belong to him. It was important for her to escape from wherever she was now. She had to leave before...before what? Try as she might, the memory remained out of reach; yet, without conscious thought, she knew whatever it was that she attempted to recall, it would change her life forever and, likely, not for the better. And not simply her life, but all those she loved.

It was several more days before she could open her eyes without experiencing the continued pain in her head and the feeling of despair plaguing her thoughts. Fortunately, today the harsh white pain had lessened substantially, and her vision had cleared. With care, she turned her head to the side to examine the room further. A variety of fragrances emanated from a large vase of flowers, which filled the gentle breeze from the open window with the scent of a spring day. She could see more than two dozen yellow roses mixed with bits of greenery. She wondered what flower was her favorite.

Turning her head to the opposite side of the room, she realized she was not alone. The same man she recalled from her first awakening sat in a nearby chair, one leg crossed over the other, a book upon his lap. His strong profile stole her breath away. Like it or not, he disturbed her. Although she had yet to view him standing, she could tell from his perfect posture, he was quite tall. His jacket, a dusty black, nearly gray, spread across his wide shoulders as if it would never tolerate a wrinkle in *ne plus ultra*. She studied his averted profile and realized he was classically handsome: His hair was the darkest of browns, but with hints of red, his brows the same rich shade of russet. His features square and angular. A strong, straight nose.

Despite the distance between them, she sensed his power — his complete control of his world. He raised his head. Their eyes met and held. Strangely enough, she could not look away. His gaze threatened to steal her breath away. His eyes were a pale silver and unsettling in a manner that had her wondering if he had judged her and found her wanting.

She knew she frowned, but she could not prevent her reaction. He had told her his name, but she could not recall it. His was not a face easily forgotten, and she was certain she did not know him. Even so, as there was no one else about, she cleared her throat to say, "Could you assist me?"

As if released from a cold winter, he rose quickly, permitting the book to drop to the floor. He immediately moved to the bed to sit upon the edge and capture her hand again. He caressed the back of it, silently studying her with close scrutiny.

"Elizabeth, my love," he said in tones speaking of relief. "Thank our dearest Lord. How do you feel?"

She swallowed hard against the panic filling her chest. He called her *Elizabeth*. Was that truly her name? Surely he would not call her such if it was not her name, but she did not feel as if the name fit her. *Elizabeth* was a most proper name. Lying in a bed while a strange man held her hand certainly did not feel proper. Could he have confused her with another? Yet, if *Elizabeth* was not her name, what was it?

"Elizabeth?" Concern marked his tone. "Tell me what ails you. Do you still have a headache? Doctor Nott promised the pain would decrease when the swelling abated."

"I do feel stronger," she assured him, although the words provided her nothing of calm. A thousand questions rushed to her lips, but she could not speak any of them aloud, for she was not certain she wished to know the answer.

"You are so pale." He caressed her cheek, and it was all she could do not to close her eyes and sigh. His touch held great tenderness.

"Where am I?" she asked, attempting to right her memory.

"In our home in London. In Mayfair. You are in the mistress's quarters."

"What happened to cause my injuries?"

She watched as indecision briefly flickered across his features before he reined in his emotions. "A carriage accident."

She attempted to keep her expression as blank as was his.

"When?"

"Nearly a week prior. Your head struck a paver stone, and you were kicked in the leg by a donkey pulling a cart. Fortunately, you incurred only a large bruise from the stubborn animal. My sister and your maid have taken turns throughout the day, massaging your legs and arms to be certain the blood does not pool because of inaction. The fact you are considered a great walker proved advantageous in this matter. We could have lost you. Everyone was so frightened."

"Including you?"

"Most assuredly. You must know—"

"But I do not," she insisted.

A muscle jerked in his jaw, and a frown creased his forehead. "I do not understand," he said after a long pause.

She stilled under his piercing gaze. "I remember nothing of this room. Of my name. Of—"

"Of me?" he demanded.

She sighed deeply, before squeezing her eyes shut for a brief moment. At length, she said, "Nothing of you either."

He quickly released her hand and stood to pace the open area. She watched as he ran his hand through his hair in what appeared to be frustration. When, at last, he turned to her, his face was in shadow. When he spoke, he enunciated each syllable carefully, as if willing her to remember. "I am your husband. William. Fitzwilliam Darcy. And you are my wife, Elizabeth Darcy."

"It cannot be—" she began, but the scowl claiming his features silenced her protest.

"This is unacceptable. I realize I was never your first choice as a husband, but it is too late to change your mind. The vows have been spoken. The registry signed. You cannot deny your pledge with this ploy. I will not have it. No matter how often you call out George Wickham's name, he will never be your husband. I will never release you."

She closed her eyes, battling the despondency pouring through her. "I know nothing of a marriage to you or a desire to marry anyone named 'George Wickham.'"

"You have called out for him twice," he stubbornly charged.

"He means nothing to me," she insisted. She struggled to conceal how much his accusation bothered her.

"But neither do I." The bitterness in his tone stabbed her conscience. "I would never have thought you capable of deception. Flippancy and pride and even prejudice, but never spitefulness."

"Please." She squeezed her eyes closed to block out his hurt expression. "I never set out to betray you." She looked upon him again, willing him to believe her. "I do not know the answers to your questions. I cannot provide you the assurances you seek."

He studied her for an elongated moment before returning to the bed and reclaiming her hand. "We will discover a means from this madness. What is it you require of me? Speak your wishes, and if it is within my power, I will grant it."

She desperately wished she could give him what he sought, but she truly had no idea how to resolve their dilemma. "I speak the truth. I wish you believed me." She turned her head so she no longer had to look upon the desolation marking his features. Thankfully, before their conversation could continue, a maid showed a kind-looking elderly gentleman into the room.

"I see our patient is awake," he said. "I am Doctor Nott, Mrs. Darcy."

Her supposed husband explained, "Mrs. Darcy appears to have lost her memory, Nott. I would have you consult with others who know more of the field of such injuries regarding her care. I wish only the best for my wife."

"I understand your concern, Mr. Darcy," the physician said with practiced patience, "but what you describe of Mrs. Darcy's condition is to be expected after such trauma. The swelling—"

"I insist," her husband said in stubborn tones.

"As you wish, sir," Nott declared. "Might I examine her first?"

"Certainly." To her, Mr. Darcy said, "I will return when

Nott is finished."

"It is not necessary," she suggested, but the look of disapproval crossing his features cut short her protest.

"It is necessary," came his dry retort.

She presented him a quick nod of acceptance, but the movement caused her to blanch white from the sharp pain claiming the front part of her head.

"Careful," Nott cautioned her. "Go, Darcy. Permit me time to examine your wife thoroughly. We will speak later."

"Mr. Darcy?" His butler, Mr. Thacker, waited politely by the door.

"Yes, Thacker." He attempted to concentrate on his business affairs, but all he could think on was what had occurred with Elizabeth.

"Mr. Cowan to see you, sir."

"Show him up, Thacker."

In less than a minute, the Bow Street Runner entered Darcy's study. Darcy stood to greet the man. "Cowan. Might I offer you a drink?"

"No thank you, sir. I fear I have but a few minutes to spare. I wished to bring you the most current information on Mr. Wickham."

Darcy sat heavily. "Tell me." His heart raced in anticipation. He did not think he could bear losing Elizabeth to any man, but especially not to his former friend, George Wickham. "What have you discovered?"

Cowan removed a small journal from an inside pocket and opened it to read. "So far, I have found no reliable witnesses who can corroborate your sighting of Mr. Wickham in London on the day of Mrs. Darcy's accident."

"But Mrs. Darcy distinctly called Mr. Wickham's name before she bolted away from my carriage," Darcy argued. "And I swear I saw him walking away from the area when I looked up at the crowd gathered about Elizabeth's unconscious state." He would never tell anyone of his wife's murmurings since her accident.

Cowan consulted his notes. "I did not say Mr. Wickham held no presence in London. Several of the man's fellow militia mates were in the City, including Captain Denney, as well as the woman Mrs. Younge. I have men watching each."

"Have there been any sightings of Wickham?" Darcy asked.

"None we can substantiate, but if Mr. Wickham is in London, I will find him."

Darcy sighed heavily. He wanted this business with Wickham and Elizabeth to end. He suspected if his old school chum had made promises to Elizabeth, another hefty donation to Wickham's purse would convince the man to leave Elizabeth to him. Darcy was not certain he could continue to adore Elizabeth as he did now, but he knew for certain he could not live one extra day if she chose to leave him. "Thank you for your diligence. Please know it is my intention to remove Mrs. Darcy to Pemberley as soon as she is well enough to travel."

"When do you anticipate that might be?" Cowan asked as he returned his journal to its proper place inside his jacket.

"Doctor Nott believes Mrs. Darcy will be fit for travel some time in the next week. Perhaps a fortnight. She must not over exhaust herself. Therefore, I have ordered the new yacht to Dover. We will travel north by sea and then across land to Pemberley."

It was two more days before she ventured from her bed. With the assistance of her maid—a woman who claimed her name was Hannah and she had been serving her for several weeks—as well as Mr. Darcy's housekeeper, Mrs. Romberg, Elizabeth was able to have a bath and a proper toilette. She was surprised when Hannah chose a gown and robe she could not imagine she would have owned, for it was satin and lace, and although she knew nothing of her past, she thought herself more likely to choose a more sensible gown.

"A gift from Mr. Darcy," Hannah explained when

Elizabeth's eyebrow rose in question.

She was settled upon the bench and Hannah was brushing her hair when a soft knock at the door announced her "husband's" presence. Despite her best efforts, her breath caught in her throat. The sheer power of his demeanor was almost too much to bear. "I am glad to see you from your bed." He approached slowly, and Elizabeth swallowed hard against the panic rising in her chest. "Might I?" He gestured to the brush Hannah held. The maid quickly handed it over. "Why do you not fetch Mrs. Darcy a shawl? I thought my wife might enjoy a bit of fresh air."

"That would be lovely," Elizabeth said softly.

Hannah curtsied and then disappeared into the bowels of the house. He motioned for Elizabeth to turn around, but she waved off the idea. "I would prefer to remain as I am."

His frown spoke his concern. "Are you still so dizzy?" He crossed behind her and applied the brush to her still damp hair.

"I am not yet steady on my feet, but that is not the reason I do not wish to turn upon the bench."

His efforts slowed. "Might you trust me enough to explain?" She could hear the caution in his tones. Since the first day when they had argued over her loss of memory, they had avoided the subject, instead spending time as do long-time friends, playing cards and his reading to her.

A sad smile claimed her lips. "I cannot bear the looking glass. It is a stranger I see staring back at me."

He came around to kneel before her, catching her hand in his. "You do not recognize yourself in the glass? Is that what you mean?"

She turned her head to glance into the mirror. "I know nothing of the woman I view before me."

He caressed her cheek. "I know the woman within and without." He brushed his lips across hers. "Permit me to chronicle the splendor of the woman I married."

Chapter 2

BEFORE HE SPOKE AGAIN, he returned to brushing her hair. "I certainly cannot style your hair as Hannah might, but I believe I can manage a braid." He divided her hair into three sections. Casually, he began his tale. "I recall the first time I viewed your hair undone. You had walked to Netherfield to visit with your sister, who had taken ill."

"I have a sister? Does she live at Netherfield?" she asked in eager tones.

"You have four sisters," he said as he began to overlap the sections of her hair. "You are the second of five. And, yes, the *former* Miss Bennet resides at Netherfield, but, in Hertfordshire. However, at that time, she had not yet married Netherfield's master, Mr. Charles Bingley."

"Then why was my sister in residence at Netherfield? Surely nothing from propriety was practiced? You are not saying my sister is a woman of loose morals?"

"Nothing of the sort," he assured. "Miss Bennet is your favorite sister. Mr. Bingley's sisters invited Miss Bennet to tea. Despite an impending storm, your mother sent your sister Jane to Netherfield on horseback."

She glanced over her shoulder at him. "You are implying something in your tone."

He admitted, "Mr. Bingley is quite wealthy and your sister is very comely. I do not know whether it was Mrs. Bennet's hope for Miss Bennet to take ill or not, but, such is neither here nor there, for Miss Bennet and Mr. Bingley are married, and, for all intents and purposes, quite happy." He gathered her hair again. "Yet, their marriage was not my intended tale. I planned to describe the first time I viewed you with your hair down. You had walked the some three miles from Longbourn, your father's estate, to Netherfield because Miss Bennet had taken ill with a fever after her wet ride the previous evening. You were announced into the morning room, where Miss Bingley and I shared the table." He paused to lean closer to her ear to whisper, "You stole both my breath and my heart in that moment. Your cheeks pink from the exercise. Your lovely eyes sparkling with humor, for, most assuredly, you realized Miss Bingley would not approve of either your skirt tails steeped six inches deep in mud or the blowsy arrangement of your hair about your shoulders. I, however, knew my earlier attempts to ignore you were fruitless."

"Why would you wish to ignore me?" she demanded.

"Such is a long story I will gladly explain in detail over the next few days, but, for now, suffice it to say I acted with misplaced pride. A man in my position and with my wealth is often pursued by families seeking a profitable match for their daughters. I had become accustomed to their deference and built my defenses against their attempts to trap me in a marriage not of my choice."

"Surely, you did not think me of that nature?" she accused. His words had her again ill-at-ease. What was she truly like before she had come to this place? Did she practice morals? Possess opinions? Was she shy or did she speak when she should not?

"At the time, I possessed no means of knowing the truth of your character, for our acquaintance was new; yet, such does not matter. My hard-honed logic had lost the battle because the most beautiful woman of my acquaintance had bewitched me: body and soul."

She found herself sucking in a breath of anticipation. Despite what he said, she could not imagine herself married to

In Want of a Wife

such a man. Were they equal in station? Part of what he said implied they were not. Yet, if her sister married a wealthy man who lived in a grand manor, then, most certainly, her family was not destitute. Did not her supposed husband just say her father also owned an estate?

She glanced up to his reflection in the mirror. In spite of her constant feeling of uncertainty, she could easily see how belonging to Fitzwilliam Darcy was something quite special. Comforting even, in an odd sort of way. The man appeared built for protection. At least, he meant to see to her welfare. Yet, an unanswered question, one that danced along the edge of her memory, but did not make an appearance, would not leave her be. It plagued her that she held no memory of the man who stood lovingly behind her, dressing her hair. However, no matter how often she had set her mind to the problem, she held no memory of having fallen in love with the man. Did she love him?

Although she assumed they had shared intimacies, she knew nothing of his touch or the taste of his kiss. "How long have we been married?"

Before he could answer a knock at the door interrupted them. "Mr. Darcy, the table and chairs you requested placed in the garden are ready, sir."

"Thank you, Mr. Thacker." He turned to her. "Permit me, my dear." And without preamble or her permission, his arms came about her. He lifted her, to cradle her against his chest. With a flutter of butterflies in her stomach, she clung to him, arms laced about his neck. For a brief second, she worried if she might prove too heavy for him, but he appeared sure-footed and not from breath as they descended the elegant staircase.

Curious, she glanced about her to discover a stately Town home, one, obviously, belonging to a wealthy man; yet, not a speck of opulence could be viewed. Fine art upon the walls. Polished marble. Thick rugs. And plenty of windows to permit the light to fill the space and to announce to the world how well-heeled the house's owner was. "It is magnificent, William," she said softly against his neck, as she nestled closer to him.

"I am pleased you approve." He kissed her forehead before shifting her weight to turn them through the door of what most certainly was his study, to cross the room and exit through open patio doors. "It remains warm for this time of year, but I asked Hannah to provide you a blanket and shawl to be certain you did not take an ague."

"You are very good to me," she said obediently.

"You are my wife," he responded, as if that fact should explain his actions, and, for a brief instant, she considered challenging him; but, then, he added, "I am eternally grateful to our Lord for not stealing you away from me. I would be lost without you in my life, Elizabeth." And, her heart instinctively called out his name. She remained so confused regarding what she should feel.

He gently placed her in a waiting chair and knelt before her to tuck a blanket across her lap. "Tell me if you become chilly."

She tilted her hand back to squint up into the weak November sun. "It feels wonderful to be outside."

He leaned in to whisper. "I recall the sprinkle of freckles across your nose when I met you quite unexpectedly upon Pemberley's lawn last August."

She eyed him suspiciously. "Pemberley?"

He smiled and dimples brightened his expression. "My home in Derbyshire."

Without considering his reaction to her response, she asked, "If I am from Hertfordshire, why was I in Derbyshire?"

The passion that had marked his smile of moments ago disappeared. "If you are marked by forgetfulness, how are you aware of geography?"

Her focus shifted quickly. "You believe I am practicing some farce," she accused. Since he had entered her quarters a half hour earlier, it had been she who had asked the questions. She had yet to set aside his previous remarks regarding her honesty, and, now, his skepticism had returned.

"Perhaps the sunshine has brought you *enlightenment*." He leaned forward to capture her chin in his large palm. "Has your mind cleared? Are you lucid enough to make your explanations to me?"

"How dare you!" she snapped, as she shoved to her feet. "I am suddenly chilled after all. I shall return to the house." She would like to say she would pack her belongings and leave, but she had no idea where she might go or how she might manage a journey on her own. Even now, she swayed in place, her vision blurry.

Immediately, he caught her to him to steady her stance. His warmth along her front offered the comfort his words did not. "I beg your forgiveness, Elizabeth," he whispered as he tightened his embrace. "My infernal pride eats away at my soul as did the eagle eat away at Prometheus's liver. I truly do not care if you have acted against me this once. I simply wish my Elizabeth — my wife — back."

She again wished to ask him to prove they were married, but she feared both the return of his anger and the method he might employ as proof. Instead, she chose a different response. "From what little I have observed of your life, I would be fortunate to be called 'wife' by you, and I truly understand the chaos you suffer, for I suffer it also. It is quite daunting to wake in an unfamiliar room with a stranger claiming me as his wife. I cannot help but to question our relationship."

"Why would I name you otherwise, if we were not faithfully married?" he countered. "What could be my purpose? You have observed the quality of my household, and, although it will sound vain to say so, many consider my countenance more than passable. What would be my motive?"

How could she explain her hesitation? He had done nothing that should cause her unease, but she experienced the emotion, nevertheless. She attempted to soften her tone when she responded. "Any woman would know pleasure at calling you 'husband.'"

"But you do not?" His eyebrow quirked higher in response.

"I seriously do not know what to feel," she protested. "What is real? You demand I accept your words as truth — to accept your honesty. Honesty from a man who *claims to be* my husband."

"*Claims to be?*" he hissed in disapproving tones. "You use that phrase quite often when you speak of our relationship."

"I would know nothing of my life if you did not tell me what you know of it." She attempted to explain the unexplainable.

His left hand drifted to the small of her back to nudge her closer. "Perhaps it is time I show you what lies between us. To teach you what to feel so you will no longer doubt the depth of our love."

"I am not certain—" she began, but a touch of his finger against her lips silenced her completely.

"I am certain," he said with what sounded of customary assurance in the truth of his words. "I wish to feel my beautiful wife tremble with anticipation and need while in my arms."

Part of her silently demanded she did not desire his kiss, but a more primitive demand overcame her rational thought. Time slowed, and the effect had nothing to do with her injury, but rather with the man who held her securely in his embrace. One imperative tapped out a single word inside her head: *His*. She was *his*, and despite a continuation of her misgivings, she knew she belonged in his arms. Heat crackled in the pit of her stomach, seeping into her most private place. It slipped deep inside her veins, sending out a demand for her to cling to him, which she did with all her might—clutching fists full of his jacket in her clenched hands.

At length, he eased the pressure of his mouth on hers, but he continued to tease and taunt her with his tongue and in a manner she had not thought possible to enjoy: He cupped her buttocks to pull her closer to his obviously enlarged manhood. It was as if he meant to demand her body bend to his wishes.

"Do you still doubt the connection we hold?" he asked on what sounded of a satisfied sigh, as his lips slid down the length of her neck.

She hesitated, fearing to admit to what his kiss had done to her. As much as she wished to surrender to what would clearly be a moment of tenderness, a part of her brain wished to rebuke his touch—to demand he tell her all he knew of her history. "I never doubted the appeal you hold," she said judiciously.

"Evidently not," he quipped, "If you still hold your doubts." He released her quickly, almost too quickly, for her legs wished to buckle. He steadied her with one hand while sweeping up the forgotten blanket with the other. "Sit," he ordered, and she did as he had instructed.

She caught his wrists to prevent him from leaving her alone. Despite her fears, she did not wish for them to know discord. He was her only connection to her past. "I apologize, William. I do not mean to place consternation upon your brow."

His expression softened. "And I do not mean to bring my lack of self control to your door."

"Doctor Nott said this inflammation of the brain would likely subside with more time," she offered in hopeful tones.

"The good physician confided as much to me," he admitted. He glanced to the house where a pretty girl waited his acknowledgement. "I thought it might do you well to speak to others. My sister Georgiana awaits to keep you company. Although she does not know all of our history, she is aware of parts of what has passed between us, and she is familiar with your Hertfordshire family. I have instructed her to answer your questions to the best of her knowledge. Holding nothing back."

"Thank you, William," she whispered. "But where will you be?"

"Just inside at my desk, addressing estate business. When you tire, ask Georgiana to summon me, and I will gladly return you to your quarters." He gently kissed her forehead. "I find I am quite addicted to having you in my arms." His thumb seductively followed the curve of her jaw. "And in my bed."

She whispered, "I shall not lie and say your kiss did not shake my resolve, but surely you wish more of our relationship than intimacies."

"I wished for a woman who complemented my strengths and my weaknesses with hers," he admitted in soft tones.

"And you believe me to be such a woman?" she asked.

A muscle jerked in his cheek. "I know you to be everything I never realized I needed in this world."

Chapter 3

SHE WAS THANKFUL HER "husband" had been called away on business, for after her conversation with Mr. Darcy's sister, Elizabeth was more confused than ever before. It was not that the girl was not obliging. On the contrary, she had liked Georgiana Darcy from the moment the girl joined her — a giggle of happiness emanating from Miss Darcy. "I am so pleased you are well enough to be from your bed. William has been so distraught, as have I," the girl said on a rush.

"I am assuming Mr. Darcy has explained my loss of memory," she suggested in kind tones.

A hint of concern crossed Miss Darcy's countenance. "I am certain William did not tell me everything. Unfortunately, my brother still views me as his 'little' sister, the one who regularly followed him about the halls of Pemberley, asking every question I could summon to keep his attention. Not that he was not most kind to me. Even with all his responsibilities, William has never denied me anything. And he has always been the most understanding of brothers."

She smiled upon the girl, who evidently wished Elizabeth to think well of Mr. Darcy. "Have you other brothers and sisters?"

"Oh, no," the girl said, her mouth turning down in obvious sadness. "My mother reportedly lost two children before I made an appearance. I have been told she knew great happiness at my birth, but as Lady Anne Darcy lived but a year following my delivery, I cannot speak to her thoughts with any assurance. It is quite disconcerting to know one's mother paid for one's existence with her life."

"Surely no one ever spoke such disparaging words to you?" Elizabeth's ire rose quickly in defense of the girl. She wondered if she often took up the cause of those who suffered at the hands of others.

"I assure you, neither father nor William made such statements," Miss Darcy said with a nod of her head in affirmation. "Even when I have acted foolishly, they have shown me nothing but their devotion and love. I am quite blessed."

"Seeing as how your brother refers to this house," Elizabeth gestured to the terrace, "as *his*, rather than *my family's*, I am assuming your father is also no longer in your family."

"Some five years past," the girl confessed. "My father held on until he knew satisfaction in William's ability to shoulder all the responsibilities of Pemberley."

The butler delivered tea and cakes, providing Elizabeth a moment to gather her thoughts before their conversation continued. When Mr. Thacker made his exit, she turned to the girl to ask, "Would you tell me what you know of my and Mr. Darcy's courtship and something of my family in Hertfordshire."

"You are certain Mr. Wickham has not departed the area?" Darcy glanced to the run-down lodging in London's East Side, where Wickham had reportedly taken up residence. He had been pleased that Cowan had located Darcy's former friend, for it proved what he knew already. The man of whom he caught a glimpse when Darcy had chased after Elizabeth on the day of her accident had actually been George Wickham.

"When he goes out it is usually to a gaming hall or to visit with his ladybird at a hotel in a more respectable area of town," Cowan assured. "My men follow him, switching off when the lieutenant appears suspicious. They wear different coats and hats and even a wig or two to keep Mr. Wickham distracted."

"I cannot comprehend what Wickham is doing in

London," Darcy confessed. "I thought Colonel Fitzwilliam saw the lieutenant and Mrs. Darcy's sister settled in Newcastle. It has not been three months since I provided the man a means to save Miss Lydia's reputation. Surely he has not deserted his post already."

"I have sent a man north to learn what we can of the reason Mr. Wickham has chosen to travel to London at the same time you have brought Mrs. Darcy to Darcy House," Cowan confirmed.

"Is Mrs. Wickham staying with him?" Darcy could not think of the former Lydia Bennet, as foolish as the chit was, having to suffer such conditions as Wickham's wife.

"Not of which we are aware. Neither the landlord nor any of the man's patrons speak of a woman in his company."

Darcy could not conceal his sigh of exasperation. "Follow him. Learn what you can of Mr. Wickham's business. Contain him if he attempts to leave London or if he shows his face anywhere near Darcy House before I successfully remove Mrs. Darcy to Derbyshire. I will inform Colonel Fitzwilliam of your search. Perhaps he can assist with any military angles you care to pursue."

As had become customary for her over the past few days, she woke to find her husband in her room, usually sitting at a small table, a breakfast tray before him and a newsprint in his hand, the heavy window drapes pulled aside to permit in the light, while her bed drapes remained closed, except for a small crack through which she could view him, and, consequently, he could keep an eye on her. He sat so straight—so proper, as if someone had drummed the stance into him, making the unnatural appear natural. Somehow his lack of relaxation both comforted and disconcerted her, at the same time. How could she ever think to fit into his world? From what Miss Darcy confided yesterday, Elizabeth suspected she could not.

Although the girl shared much the same information as had Mr. Darcy, the reality of Miss Darcy's words rang truer, for the girl knew not the sophistication to practice guise. Therefore, last evening, Elizabeth had made the effort to accept what Miss Darcy had shared. *I am Elizabeth Bennet Darcy, formerly of Longbourn in Hertfordshire. I am married to Fitzwilliam Darcy, whose mother was the daughter of an earl, and whose father named a noble line of ancestors. While I am a gentleman's daughter, my father, a simple man, holds no claim to fame or fortune.*

Evidently, from Miss Darcy's report, Elizabeth had refused Mr. Darcy's initial proposal, a fact she could not fathom, for, from what Hannah had shared, the gentleman held a reputed income of some ten thousand a year. That fact alone should have settled the matter between them. A man with ten thousand a year had to be pursued by women at every turn, but, somehow, Mr. Darcy had chosen her, a fact that mystified her.

"You are awake," he said, and she turned her head in time to note a frown of what appeared to be concern cross his countenance before he brought his expression under control.

"I am." After brushing the hair from her face, she lifted her weight higher into the bed. "You are an early riser."

He pushed the bed drapes aside. "I keep country hours even in London. I pray that does not bother you."

"If your sister's chronicle of my life is true, I, obviously, prefer early mornings, as well," she responded.

"I pray Georgiana's willingness to assist you to health did not overwhelm you." He crossed to the bell cord. "I will order fresh tea and toast. Do you think to require more?"

"Such will do for the moment," she said in light tones. Instinctively, she arched an eyebrow in his direction and immediately wondered how he might meet her pertness. Thankfully, he appeared to accept her doing so with a slight smile. "But I assume a lady may change her mind if she wishes."

His smile deepened. "It pleases me to hear the return of a bit of playfulness in your words. Your bedevilments were one of the things that attracted me to you."

"Miss Darcy says you described many of our early conversations in some detail in your letters to her," she ventured. "I would say bedevilment is too kind of a term for my previous

In Want of a Wife

impertinence."

"In most cases, I deserved your rebukes, but, now, we hold a better understanding," he assured.

"Do we?" she asked.

He watched her intently. "We each know the other's secrets," he said in even tones. "I believe we are stronger because of our earlier misunderstandings."

She ran her suddenly sweaty palms across the bed linen. "Even if I cannot remember all that transpired between us?"

He sat upon the bed's edge to capture her hand. "Marriage is forever, Elizabeth. Even if your memory does not return, we must go forward. Doctor Nott assures me you are otherwise healthy and should recover from the stiffness and the bruises within a week or two. We can still have a full life together."

"And what of my family?" she asked softly, as she attempted to take in all he said.

"Do you wish to know more of the Bennets?"

She admitted, "After speaking to Miss Darcy yesterday, I wondered why none of my family had called upon me."

"Your Aunt and Uncle Gardiner called several times while you were unconscious," he explained. "Once we discovered your infirmity, your Uncle Gardiner and I agreed with Doctor Nott's diagnosis that exposing you too quickly to too many people you did not recognize would only cause you more harm. If you are prepared to speak to the Gardiners, I will dispatch a message to them right away."

"Do I enjoy the Gardiners?" she asked tentatively.

"You and Mrs. Bingley are the Gardiners' favorites among your sisters. I suspect the feelings are reciprocated," he disclosed.

"Do you approve of the Gardiners?" she asked pointedly.

"I admit there was a time I did not think I would care for them, but I found I always enjoy my conversations with both your aunt and uncle. Mr. Gardiner is well read, and Mrs. Gardiner spent much of her youth less than five miles from my ancestral estate. We share many points in common."

Before she could continue their conversation, a maid

answered his ring for service. After giving the woman specific instructions, he reached out to lift Elizabeth from her bed. "I will set you down in your dressing room so you might see to your personal needs. Know I will be near if you require my assistance. Do not hesitate to call out if you feel dizzy or the like. Hannah has laid out your robe and slippers."

"Do you not have more pressing business, Mr. Darcy?" she asked as she slipped her arms about his neck, while marveling at how comfortable she felt in his embrace, especially as she had no memory of him beyond this last week.

"You are the only pressing business I care to address, Elizabeth. You are the woman I adore."

A telltale heat pinked her cheeks. "Although I appreciate the sentiment, I still hold no memory of our life before I woke in this house. Now, I borrow memories from you and your sister."

He set her upon her feet. "I wish things were different for you—for us. God means to test us, but I have no doubt you will persevere. We will come out of this stronger. Now, see to your ablutions, and we will continue our conversation over breakfast." Making certain she was steady on her feet, he backed from the room.

Elizabeth glanced to her reflection in the small mirror upon a nearby table. Her hair was a mess and her skin pale. She wondered for a brief moment why Mr. Darcy had not said anything regarding her appearance. "Because he is too much of a gentleman," she whispered as she poured water from the ewer into a bowl and bent to splash the tepid liquid upon her face. "And he claims to love me." The idea brought a brief smile to her lips before the thought of where declarations of love might lead them.

A flush of color pinked her complexion. "Oh, my," she murmured. "Husband and wife."

She used another splash of water to cool her cheeks. Swallowing hard, she set her shoulders in a straight line. She was not certain what she meant to do about the six foot plus virile male in the adjoining bedchamber, but she would—what did he term it—persevere. Quickly finishing her ablutions, she donned her robe and slippers and ran a comb through her hair before bracing her weight against the various pieces of furniture to reach the door. Her legs wished to buckle, but she demanded their participation until she reached the door. "Mr. Darcy, I could use a strong arm upon which to lean."

He was on his feet immediately and crossing the room to reach her. "Permit me." He meant to lift her into his arms again, but she stayed his hand.

"I would prefer to challenge my legs," she instructed.

"I should have expected nothing less," he said in seductive tones, while anchoring her hand against his side. "I told Hannah to remain close in case you required her care," he shared. Sitting her in a straight-backed chair at the small table, he gestured to the offerings. She suddenly realized she was quite famished. "Do you wish me to pour your tea?"

She lifted her hand to show him the slight tremble found there. "It might be best." She made herself smile at him when a frown marked his forehead. "Your doing so will permit me to view how much you know of my breakfast preferences."

He bowed elegantly. "I am your knight, my lady." With those words he set about preparing her a cup of tea with a splash of milk and a sliver of sugar from the brick. He presented her the tea and went about spreading a berry conserve upon a thick slice of toasted bread.

His fingers fascinated her. Like his posture, his movements were precise and perfect. She suspected if she had prepared the toast with jam, the berry mixture would be unevenly spread and likely dripping off the edge on one side, but not his presentation. The toast he placed before her was covered uniformly, all the way to the edges. She had married England's "perfect" man. The idea brought a giggle rushing to her lips, but she covered her reaction with a cough.

Taking a sip of the tea and finding it—what else—*perfect*, she asked, "You never told me why you originally objected to my uncle."

He did not answer until he returned to his chair. "My presumptions," he clipped, "are not something of which I am proud." He paused briefly. "In truth, I have been a selfish being all my life, in practice, though not in principle. As a child, I was taught what was *right*; but I was not taught to correct my temper. I was given good principles, but left to follow them in pride and conceit. Unfortunately, as an only son—for many years an only *child*—I was spoilt by my parents, who, though good themselves—my father, particularly, was all that was benevolent and amiable—allowed, encouraged, almost taught me to be selfish and overbearing—to care for none beyond my own family circle, to think meanly of all the rest of the world, to *wish* at least to think meanly of their sense and worth compared with my own. Such I was, from eight to eight-and-twenty; and such I might still have been but for you, dearest, loveliest Elizabeth! What do I not owe you! You taught me a lesson, hard indeed at first, but most advantageous. By you I was properly humbled. You showed me how insufficient were all my pretensions to please a woman worthy of being pleased."

"That does not speak specifically to your objection to the Gardiners," she insisted.

"In my former pomposity, I assumed a man who lived in close proximity to his warehouses lacked quality," he admitted. A frown reappeared upon his features.

"Then my uncle is in trade?"

"Mr. Gardiner owns a large and profitable import-export business."

It was her turn to frown. "From Miss Darcy's description of my family, I assumed I was a gentleman's daughter. Mr. Bennet and Mr. Gardiner are not blood relations?"

"Mr. Gardiner is brother to Mrs. Bennet and to Mrs. Philips, whose husband practices law in the village located just outside of your father's estate."

"Now I understand what Miss Darcy appeared to have difficulty sharing. Though my father is a gentleman, our connections are not equal in any way."

"I wish Georgiana had not approached the subject," he said with a sad shake of his head.

"I insisted," she confessed. "Do not blame Miss Darcy."

"Nevertheless, I would not have you fretting over something long settled between us," he said authoritatively.

She chose not to continue to argue with him. She suspected such was best in dealing with this particular gentleman. Although he appeared eager to cater to her needs, she doubted his opinions were easily changed once he had set his mind to a course. She imagined the responsibilities that rested upon his shoulders demanded he take a commanding tone with all with whom he dealt. Instead, she summarized, "You will permit the Gardiners to call upon me?"

"Certainly," he repeated in what sounded of cautious tones.

Therefore, she suggested, "It would please me if you would make yourself available during their call." Another thought caught her, and so she asked, "I did not inquire as to where the Gardiners live. Will visiting me be an imposition for them?"

"Not far," he confided. "In Cheapside. On Milk Street."

She nodded her understanding, but she possessed only a general idea of how Cheapside was part of London. "And my family?"

"Mr. Bennet and I have exchanged daily expresses regarding your recovery. I will write to him now and ask him to come to London. I would expect him tomorrow. I know he is very worried over your health. The only thing keeping him in Hertfordshire has been his concern for how his appearance in London might affect you."

Again, she mentally prepared herself for what would likely be an emotional meeting. "You will speak to Mr. Bennet of my unusual condition?"

"I have done so previously, but I will write again of your tender convalescence. I am certain your father will act prudently," he assured. "However, if you like, I will remain close."

It was odd to trust this man above all others, but what choice did she have. As it appeared she was his wife, no one would act against him to remove her from his care. Therefore, it must be as he said earlier: They must carve out a life together. That brought her back to the idea of the need for intimacies between them.

"I have another request," she said with as much determination as she could muster. He nodded for her to proceed. "I was wondering if you would consider a period of courtship between us. I would appreciate time to learn more of the man with whom I am to spend the remainder of my days."

"A courtship?" he asked skeptically. "What kind of courtship? Living separately? My calling on you, bringing you flowers and what not?"

She thought that would be lovely, but from the tone of his voice, she doubted he would agree. "Nothing so drastic," she assured.

"I will not be the laughing stock of London, Elizabeth," he warned. "I must maintain appearances or else those with whom I do business will think me an easy mark," he contested.

"No one needs to know," she insisted.

"Then what do you propose?" he questioned.

"I truly had not thought much upon it," she admitted.

His brow crinkled. "You are thinking of intimacies, are you not?"

Instinctively, she shrugged away his accusation. "I am certain each day there are thousands of women in England who willingly admit their husbands, who are strangers in every way, to their beds, but I would prefer our joining to be more than duty. Do not you?"

He took his time in replying, as if choosing his words carefully. "I want the Elizabeth Bennet I knew in my bed during the first week of marriage. That woman suited me well."

"How do I know if I can be that woman again?" She turned to study him.

"I could teach you," he offered.

"No doubt," she assured. "Yet, do you not wish me to come willingly into your embrace?"

Another long pause followed. At length, he exhaled sharply. "I promise not to press you to give yourself to me again, at least, until we reach Pemberley."

She swallowed hard. "When will that be?"

"We will not depart until you have had a reunion with your family, and then we will set out for Dover. I requested the yacht be brought around. I do not like the traffic on the Thames."

"A yacht?" she asked.

"*Lizzy's Delight*," he said with a smile.

"Named for me?" Surprise laced her tone.

"Who else?" he responded. "We will take the yacht north to Lincolnshire, and then go over land to Derbyshire. Doing so will save us several days. Yet, between your injury and the condition of the roads this time of year, I have no doubt our journey will be extended." He paused again. "Between the visit by your father, who will, I am certain, wish to remain with you for several days, at least, and the journey, I would estimate two weeks before returning to Pemberley House."

She nodded her understanding.

He stood then, as if their negotiations were over, and for a brief second she wondered whether he would order his solicitor to draw up legal papers for her to sign. "I will send Hannah in to assist you in dressing. If you are feeling well enough, please join me in my study. I would take great pleasure in showing you part of the history into which you have married."

"I would like that very much," she said with a slow smile.

"As would I. I have dreamed of our sharing such moments — with finally having someone with whom to share the responsibilities."

"To no longer be alone," she whispered. She, too, was alone. She knew that feeling firsthand.

He sighed heavily. He bent to kiss the top of her head, before lifting her chin with two fingers, so he might speak to her honestly. "I have promised not to press you for intimacies at this time, but I did not promise to leave you to your own devices. I will be spending numerous hours in your company, and I will be sleeping in the same bed as my wife. Set your mind to it, Elizabeth."

Chapter 4

DARCY HAD SAT IN the corner of the room, pretending either to read letters of business or reading for pleasure as his wife's relations attempted, with no success, to jar Elizabeth's memory. Neither the Gardiners nor her father could engage her in a conversation long enough for Elizabeth's defenses to slip. Therefore, his doubts, although not absent completely, took a large step to the rear. He was beginning to believe something greater than her being knocked to the ground, as she rushed from his hold upon her waist, had happened on the day of her accident. He had wished repeatedly over the previous two weeks that he had been aware of the comings and goings of those upon the street outside his Town house, rather than to be mesmerized by his wife's lovely countenance as he lifted her from his coach. Unfortunately, he remained too besotted with the feel of her body beneath his fingers to know anything but her on that crisp November morning.

With her family, Elizabeth attempted to assure the distraught-looking Thomas Bennet that she would soon know health. Such was one of the reasons Darcy had begun to think her memory loss was not a farce to distract him from her efforts to leave him, for, if she were pretending, the pleading inflections her father attempted to remove from his words and the manner in which Mr. Bennet held her hand would have convinced the Elizabeth that Darcy knew to admit her perfidy, rather than to torment her father thusly.

"I wish I had never asked to see my father," she had lamented as she snuggled deeper into his embrace when he joined her in her bed the evening of the first day of Mr. Bennet's visit. "I thought perhaps my viewing his face would set everything to rights, but all my selfishness did was to bring him more pain. Did he always have lines of worry about his eyes?"

Darcy recognized how the news of Elizabeth's condition would have affected Mr. Bennet, but even he had been surprised by the man's frail condition when Mr. Bennet entered Darcy House. Yet, he said, "Your father regularly sits up late into the evening to read his books and then rises early to address estate business. I am certain his doing so must affect his appearance. If you were still at Longbourn, the changes would be slow coming, and you would most likely not take note."

"You are being kind," she whispered against his skin.

He was so thankful she did not shun his touch. He had agreed, in theory, for the time being, for them not to share intimacies, but it was very difficult for him not to roll her to her back and take his pleasure from her body. Yet, the nagging question remained: Did Elizabeth ask for a period of courtship because she absolutely required it to heal or was she postponing further intimacies with him because she wanted those of another? Darcy wished he was of a stronger nature; however, he had lost all reason when he gave himself permission to know hope with their love. Therefore, he was incapable of stifling his words. "How do you know I am the type to show kindness, if you have no memory of me?"

She sighed heavily and rolled away from him, presenting him her back. "Have we returned to your doubts again? I had hoped we had opened another door."

Darcy turned to stare up at the pattern of the bed's drape. "Did you wish us to open another door, Elizabeth? To attempt to discover happiness together?"

After a long pause—one longer than he would have preferred, she said, "I thought this matter was decided between us."

Darcy released a slow calculated breath. Despite wishing for nothing more than to move forward with this woman as his wife, a nagging doubt in the form of a brief mention by the hotel clerk of a note delivered to Elizabeth — a note she never mentioned to him while they were in Bath or afterwards on the journey to London that still plagued him. He could not help but wonder if the note was from Wickham, and they planned a rendezvous. "It is," he repeated through tight lips.

"Then why do you continue to question me?" she demanded.

"I do not know," he confessed. "None of what has occurred makes sense. We were happy together for five days. At least, I was happy, and I thought you were also, but then you bolted from my arms to chase after the figure of a man I thought was settled in Newcastle with your sister Lydia."

"Mr. Wickham?" she questioned.

Just the mention of his former schoolmate always disturbed Darcy's breathing. There was nothing about the man of which he could approve. "Yes. What do you know of the man?"

"Up until my father's visit, very little beyond your previous accusations," she admitted in what sounded of reluctance. "Mrs. Bingley took time to share something of each of my sisters. She privately disclosed information of Lydia's elopement with Mr. Wickham and your part in saving my family's reputation."

"I did not act solely to earn your affection," he was quick to say. "I simply could not bear to view you so distraught when I possessed the means to resolve your misery."

"Jane made that particular fact perfectly clear," she disclosed. "My sister said you attempted to disguise your participation in the scheme, making it appear as if Uncle Gardiner financed the Wickhams' joining, but Lydia let news of your attending the wedding slip, and I wrote to Aunt Gardiner, who confirmed your continued devotion to me, for, obviously, you would not have become involved otherwise."

"The tears in your eye when you shared the news with me

demanded I act with honor. I could not permit you to suffer," he admitted.

She rolled to her side to look upon him. "Although I hold no memory of your efforts to discover my sister in London, you must permit me to thank you, in the name of all my family, for the generous compassion which induced you to take on so much trouble, and bear so many mortifications, all the sake of discovering an ill-advised couple."

"There is no reason for your family's gratitude." He reached for her hand and cupped it against his chest. Would there ever be a day when he could resist her closeness? "That the wish of giving happiness to you might add force to the other inducements which led me on, I shall not attempt to deny. But your family owes me nothing. I thought only of you."

⁂

"You are well, my love?" he inquired.

She examined the ribbons holding her reticule closed. "Why should I not be?"

"Just reassuring myself." She stared at him, a look of disapproval, one demanding he not return to questions regarding her health. Darcy wished she understood his total devotion to her. At length, he sighed heavily. "Forgive me. My esteemed father was most adamant regarding my protection of our family."

"Forgiven." A swift smile graced her lips.

Dear God, he had missed her unexpected smiles. Unable to resist, he switched his seat to sit beside her and gathered her into his arms. "I adore your smiles," he whispered, before he claimed her lips with his. A minute or so later, he released her, taking some pride in how she clung to him and how her lips were swollen from his kisses. "I thought perhaps you knew apprehension regarding traveling by ship," he confessed.

"On the contrary," she said as she straightened her bonnet.

He returned to the rear-facing seat. "Not even a few qualms?"

She stiffened, regarding him with a familiar twist of her lips. "A few, perhaps, for I have no knowledge of having ever been aboard a ship. Or traveled to Kent, for that matter."

"You have been to Kent," he said with a smile. "It was at my aunt's estate that I first proposed to you."

"First proposed?" Her curiosity piqued.

"You turned me down flat. Considered me an absolute prig!"

"Why?"

"My pride again," he admitted. "I often permitted it to cloud my opinions of others. You took me to task. Even my fortune could not persuade you to abandon your principles. That was last April. I spent several months attempting to become a better man. When you traveled to Derbyshire with the Gardiners, I was set upon proving to you I had taken your advice to heart."

She studied him for several elongated moments, as if she was digesting what he had told her. "And the ship?"

"For your information, Mr. Bennet informed me you have only ever traveled by coach—often to London to visit with the Gardiners and a half dozen times to Scotland to keep company with your father's relations," he explained. "With your injury you could have no way of knowing one way or the other." He attempted to disguise his wariness, but he feared he had failed.

"But do you not see?" A hint of concern reflected in her steady gaze. "For weeks, I have attempted to recapture my past. This journey marks my future, and I am excited to be free of the burden of my injury."

"Then I am exceedingly pleased to be sharing this one with you."

"Promise me we shall have other adventures. Memories I can claim as my own," she pleaded.

"If it were in my power, I would give you both your old memories and assist you in claiming new ones. You are my world, Elizabeth."

"Oh, Hannah, you are here," his wife exclaimed when he showed her to their quarters upon the yacht. "I am so pleased. I thought perhaps you remained at Darcy House, and I would be required to learn something of a different maid."

"No, ma'am." The girl shot a glance to him for permission to speak openly, to which he nodded his agreement. "Mr. Darcy brought me along from Pemberley to attend you. I be quite honored, ma'am."

"Hannah served Miss Darcy when my sister was young, up until our father's passing, but, when Georgiana departed for school, Hannah requested to remain at Pemberley, for her family lives near the estate. When you visited my estate in Derbyshire last August, Georgiana noticed Hannah assisting you. The two of you got on well, and before our wedding, you requested Hannah as your lady's maid. I brought her to Hertfordshire to serve you."

His wife's eyes studied Hannah's face, and he noted a slight frown marked Elizabeth's forehead. She was attempting to look for lapses in his story. "My Aunt Gardiner mentioned that her maid served the two of us when we visited the Peak District. When did I have a need of your services in Derbyshire?"

"I be assisting my uncle at the Lambton inn—The Rose and Crown. You stayed there with the Gardiners during your time in the area," Hannah explained.

"But I thought you were in Mr. Darcy's employ?" Elizabeth questioned.

"I was for many years. When Miss Darcy was very small, the late Mr. Darcy thought I might keep her company and play games with her. It be to my advantage as much as that of Miss Darcy, for I learned my letters and counting and something of manners right along with the young miss. I remained in the nursery with her until a governess was brought in." The maid chuckled lightly. "I pray the master will forgive my saying so, but Miss Darcy be afeared of her own shadow when she be a wee one. The former Mr. Darcy wished the young miss to have a companion of sorts with her at all times, and I be nearly five years Miss Darcy's senior. I learned how to dress the young miss's hair and to tend her clothes from the maid Miss Darcy had before Milly." Hannah again nodded to him. "When Miss Darcy begins spending the main part of her days in London, I

In Want of a Wife

begged the master to permit me to return to Pemberley and my family. My father be quite ill at the time. He passed some two years ago. When my mourning was over and I could return to Pemberley, they be no openings for a maid of any sort until you be kind enough to engage me. I be most appreciative, ma'am. You saved me. My uncle means to marry soon. His new wife has two daughters, who will take on my former duties at the inn."

"Thank you for the explanation," Elizabeth said with a nod of approval for the maid's sake. "I am pleased we could continue our time together." She glanced around the quarters with some uncertainty. "Does the rocking of the ocean bother you?" his wife asked innocently, and Darcy noted the death-grip she had on the back of the chair.

Instead of speaking to Elizabeth's newfound disinclinations, Darcy spoke to her previous determination. Thankfully, her injury had not robbed her of her personality completely: He knew from experience his wife would be quick to accept a challenge. "Mrs. Darcy made no complaints with the row boat or climbing the ladder to the deck. I was quite proud of her adventurous spirit."

"Very good, ma'am," Hannah pronounced.

Elizabeth repeated, "And you do not notice the rocking of the ship upon the waters?"

"My father was a fisherman, ma'am. He spent the best part of each year out on a fishing dogger somewhere between Northumberland and Denmark. I grew up in the bow of a boat, as those in my family say. My mother was employed in the kitchens at Pemberley. We had a small cottage not too far removed. All my brothers either followed my father or worked upon the estate as grooms and such."

Elizabeth appeared to swallow her unease. She accepted Hannah's explanation with a nod.

"That will be all for now," he instructed. Darcy waited until the maid disappeared into the passageway. When they were alone, he purposely edged behind his wife, tugging Elizabeth against his body. He whispered in her ear, "I could serve as

37

your anchor, my lady, just as I did when you climbed the ladder. You will discover I am quite immovable, except where you are concerned."

He noted she glanced to the bed before shoving her way from his loose embrace. "I do not require an anchor, sir," she said in testy tones. "Anchors hold things in place."

"I see." He dropped his hands to his side. She had him turned every which way: One moment she was loving and speaking of hope, and the next, she appeared barely to tolerate his touch. "Such is a sad state," he continued. "For I certainly require my wife's return. For too long I have felt adrift, that is, until you came into my life. I have prayed to serve you equally as well in this new venture as you have served me in righting my life."

Darcy had known satisfaction on their journey to Pemberley, for Elizabeth had accepted his unspoken challenge and had quickly adjusted to traveling by sea, as well as to the unpredictable delays they encountered in the northern shires. If not for the occasional hesitancy he noted crossing her expression when he professed his love for her, he would have thought the woman sitting across from him was the woman whose heart he had won after so many months of misery.

Perhaps I should withhold an acknowledgement of my affections, he thought as he watched the sleepy nod of her head while his coach rolled closer to Pemberley. *Treat her as I might if ours were a marriage of convenience.* But if he were honest with himself, Darcy did not want to treat her with indifference. During their short courtship, they had shared more than a few passionate kisses, and their first week as husband and wife had often left him breathless with desire. How could he take a step backward when all he wanted was to glory in the love she had openly declared previously?

"Where are we?" she asked as she rolled her neck several times to loosen her muscles after sleeping with her head resting against the side of the carriage.

"About ten miles from the outer land of Pemberley," he shared.

"Perhaps two hours then." She slid across the bench to peer out the coach's window. "I wish I could recall my previous visit to what will be my future home. What if I do not prove a proper mistress for the estate? Did my mother instruct me on how to go about serving my husband?"

"I would imagine Mrs. Bennet provided you with knowledge of how best to proceed," he said tactfully. As Mrs. Bennet never oversaw a proper education for her daughters, his dubiety regarding Elizabeth's assuming her position remained intact, but he would not speak of it, at this time. He had always assumed she would conquer whatever shortcomings she possessed. Her excellent insights more than compensated for what his wife lacked in actual experience.

"Then it is possible I might fail?" Sadness marked her features.

Darcy moved across the seat to sit beside her and to capture her hand. "Elizabeth, I require more than a mistress of my estate. There has been no Mrs. Darcy for more than fifteen years, and the walls of Pemberley have not fallen down into disrepair. Mrs. Reynolds and Mr. Nathan are very efficient in their oversight of Pemberley House. Even if you never excel in that capacity, I will have no complaints. I believe you will succeed, but my affection for you is not dependent upon your triumph."

"Then what role do you envision I shall play in your life?" she demanded.

Darcy attempted to vocalize what he knew by instinct. "I fear what I say will frighten you further," he admitted.

She eyed him suspiciously. "I would hear your thoughts, nonetheless."

Before he spoke, he laced their fingers. "You will think much of what I say foolish," he prefaced. An awkward pause followed, before he continued, "My revered father once declared he had often fallen in love, but always with the same woman. I hope to do likewise. I wish to know someone who will forgive me when I act foolishly and expect a like forgiveness of me in return. To have a person love me despite my imperfections. I wish to know a woman who can profess her love without the ability to name a reason for such love filling her heart. I wish the ability to concoct numerous occasions to shower said woman with my reasons for adoring her. Finally, when I pass, I want the memory of thousands of moments that speak to our love story to go out into the universe."

Chapter 5

HER HUSBAND. THE WORDS zinged through Elizabeth's brain. Inherently, she knew their marriage had to be true. So many people had gone to such lengths to convince her of the situation. Certainly, he could have paid them to do so, for, obviously, *her husband* was as wealthy as he and the others claimed. First, Darcy House's splendor. Then the sleek yacht. And, now, Pemberley with its understated elegance. But how could she have earned the affection of such a great man? Her meeting with her father proved Mr. Bennet was a "gentleman," and she, therefore, a gentleman's daughter, but as far as she could determine, such was the only thing she and Mr. Darcy had in common. Her father had actually stated that his income was but a fifth of *her husband's*. Moreover, Mr. Darcy was so handsome; she had no doubt many women pursued him. Since waking to find herself at Darcy House, upon several occasions, Elizabeth had taken an accounting of her features in a looking glass, and she knew without a doubt, she was no great beauty.

She stifled the shiver of awareness shooting up her spine. Without looking up from her plate, she knew Fitzwilliam Darcy watched her. Was he doing so because he still did not believe she possessed no memory of their time together? Or was it because he meant every word he said to her in the carriage? She bit her bottom lip in hesitation and raised her eyes to meet his.

Why would he not drop his gaze?

He leaned closer to whisper in her ear. "I never thought I would know the day you would grace my table with your presence."

"You thought me indifferent?" she asked, but they were interrupted when a servant appeared to remove the first course and replace it with the fish. She was thankful he had not responded, for she was not certain she wished to know something of how she had treated him previously. Elizabeth had the feeling she had not performed as she should have. Therefore, she directed their conversation to the estate. "How large is the property?"

With a slight frown, her husband dutifully spoke of his ancestral home. Most assuredly, his words were laced with pride, but from what she had seen, he had a right to be proud. He ended with a return of his earlier thoughts. "All the estate requires is a mistress." He caressed the back of her hand.

Elizabeth swallowed hard. She had not forgotten his promise not to claim intimacies until they reached Pemberley, and now they were at his home.

William leaned toward her, causing a tingle of awareness to race down her spine. She raised her eyes to meet his, and, instantly, her mouth ran dry. The lingering sincerity of his words and his gaze marked her as his. For a brief moment, she prayed once again to be the woman who earned his devotion, if only to continue to be the center of his attentions. Elizabeth could not discount the fact his handsome countenance did odd things to her heart. He fascinated her, and she could not account for the strange sense of comfort she experienced when she was at his side.

Even as she thought it, she became annoyed by her reaction to him. How could she imagine a complete stranger in the role of her protector? *Of her husband?*

He caressed the side of her cheek with the back of his fingers. "To answer your earlier question, there was a time you showed no particular interest in my finer qualities," he said in what sounded of a tease. Heat seared through her from his light caress to her very soul. Then he leaned closer to brush her lips with his. "And now, each day I thank our Lord for bringing you into my life."

Darcy noted a flicker of uncertainty crossing her features before she hid her thoughts behind a weak smile, plainly meant to pacify him. "Even with my loss of memory?" she asked.

"My affection would remain even if your 'loss of memory' was meant to temper my desire for you," he said softly.

"This is not a farce I practice," she hissed.

Before he responded, with a flick of his wrist, Darcy gestured his servants from the room. When they were alone, he said, "My remark was not meant as an accusation, rather, as assurance in my belief that we can face any obstacle as long as we are together." He paused to study her expression. "I feared my previous ardor, when we were alone together at Bath, might have frightened you. I should have had better control of my actions."

"Would you not have known whether such was true or not?" she instantly protested.

"When we first came together, you appeared to return my desires. I had hoped for a loving relationship," he admitted. In fact, the night before her accident, Elizabeth had initiated their coming together, tantalizing him with a satin nightgown that left little to the imagination. It was only the next morning while they shared their breakfast and in the carriage to London that she had appeared distracted. At the time, he had thought she had been embarrassed by her boldness in the bedchamber, but since her accident, he had learned of a letter delivered to his wife while he was seeing to their account and checking on the coach's readiness. Hannah had privately reported that her mistress appeared quite upset by the contents of the letter and had burned it after reading it. Now, he was left to wonder over what it entailed.

She took a second sip of her wine, evidently to provide herself time to formulate a response. "In truth, I possess no means of knowing anything of my previous actions to our intimacies, but I have no reason not to believe you when you describe our devotion to each other. Moreover, in my estimation, I do not think of myself as the timid sort. I believe the manner in which I clung to you after our kiss should be proof of my need for you in my life."

Darcy wished he could completely ignore his doubts and accept her words for what they were, but there was a part of him that would always doubt that anyone could love him as he needed to be loved. Over more years than he cared to admit, he prayed each day for someone to fill the loneliness that plagued his days. The problem remained: His head told him never to trust anyone. He had trusted George Wickham, and his former friend had betrayed him time and time again. Meanwhile, his heart demanded he simply cherish Elizabeth and ignore her calling Wickham's name in the mix of her delusions. Which emotion would win out only God knew for certain. "Despite your lack of indifference, I would prefer to be more to you than simply the man who offers his name and his protection."

It bothered him when she flinched, although the movement was barely perceptible. The action indicated what could only be her vulnerability, which had him again questioning his instincts. When it came to Elizabeth Bennet Darcy, all he would ever want was to is claim all of her as his.

"I wish I could promise you more of myself than I have." She reached for his hand, interlacing their fingers. He noted the nervousness lurking behind the fine eyes, which had long ago bewitched him body and soul.

Darcy easily recalled his first sight of her. He had been knocked sideways by her exuberance—his initial reaction an unusual stirring of desire. He had thought his response was only one of a male to the sight of a beautiful woman. In hindsight, he wondered why it was Elizabeth Bennet who created such a response in him, for neither her sister nor Miss Bingley, both beautiful women, brought forth a desire to claim them intimately. Yet, even now, after knowing her as his wife, he could not explain why the sight of her had been so thoroughly branded upon his soul, never to be erased.

"Does this sudden hesitation have something to do with

my promise to wait to claim you until we reached Pemberley? Did you think it would take longer to be at our home?" Darcy attempted to keep an accusatory tone from coloring his words.

Wariness marked the lines around Elizabeth's mouth, and she withdrew her hand from his. "I do not fear you, William," she said softly. Although she held his steady gaze, she stiffened. Something resembling dread crossed her expression.

"Then it is my touch you avoid," he corrected. He could not name what it was about him that prompted him to provoke her. Darcy suspected it was jealousy. Perhaps it was the continued look of unguarded peril found within her eyes. Or perhaps his negotiation skills had found a point of weakness, and he meant to exploit it. Perhaps he simply needed to learn whether or not her memory loss was an act. Likely, it was only the lust that had marked his days since claiming Elizabeth Bennet's acquaintance.

"Most women know qualms at the prospect of sharing intimacies for the first time," she argued in halting tones.

"However, it would not be your first time," he countered.

She placed her linen serviette upon the table. "I suppose I should ask your pardon for my leaving the table early so I might prepare for your company later." Outrage laced her tone.

He leaned toward her and noted the quick hitch of her breathing. That damnable inner voice announced she was not immune to him. "I would welcome your agreement. However, I do not want you to lie upon the bed and permit what you name as my ardor. I want the Elizabeth who welcomed me with her encouragements."

"That woman no longer exists," she protested.

The unanticipated silence between them was marred by her shoving her chair backward. Her gaze locked with his—her brilliant hazel eyes turning a dark gray. Quickly, she reclaimed her evident indifference to him. "I am your wife, and I will perform my duties to you as the mistress of your house, as well as in the marriage bed."

Defiantly, he rose and extended his hand to her. She had dared him, what else could he do, but respond, thusly? "An excellent choice."

Elizabeth placed her fingers into his open palm and stood. He ushered her from the room, instructing Mr. Nathan to have a tray with the remaining courses sent to their joint sitting room. They climbed the stairs in silence. Darcy noted how Elizabeth held herself quite royally, in the likes of Anne Boleyn climbing the stairs to the executioner's block. Whatever existed between them simmered beneath the surface. Even if his wife's memory loss was true, she could not deny the awareness they shared of each other.

Reaching the door to her quarters, he paused. She turned to look up at him, confusion skittering across her features. Darcy could not explain what happened next. The voice in his head demanded he reclaim this woman as his wife—as his lover. Surely, she could not forget the perfection of their coming together. Then again, maybe he simply surrendered to the temptation she presented. Mayhap her denials spurred him on. Or, perhaps, some Norman ancestor, whose blood ran through him, demanded that Darcy take control of his household and his marriage—announcing that Darcy had presented this woman too much power over him. Whatever the reason, he pulled her into his embrace and lowered his head to take her mouth in a kiss of absolute demand.

The spark of recognition he had felt their wedding night reared its head again. He had not mistaken her previous surrender. Knowledge of their rightness flickered briefly and then sank quickly into his gut, growing hotter by the second. The control for which he was well known melted away before it had a chance to offer an objection. Did he possess her, or did she possess him? Did it matter? As long as they remained together.

Elizabeth felt his dominance over her the instant his lips met hers. One moment all she felt was anger, and the next, she wished to melt into him and never come out. Although she held no memory of their previous intimacies, she doubted her husband had previously kissed her with such raw passion, and all she could do was cling to him. She prayed she would not physically explode from the fire rushing through her veins. If he chose to lay her on the floor of the passageway and have his way with her for all the world to view, she doubted she would verbalize a protest.

Unfortunately, or fortunately, depending upon one's perspective, the instant her obvious capitulation registered in her brain, she began to fight for control. With a cry of distress, she wriggled her way from his arms. Doing so, she felt as if she had lost part of herself, but she managed to take a step backward. However, making such a sacrifice—for that was what a separation from her husband's embrace was: a sacrifice— offered no relief, and so she stumble-stepped backward again. At length, she could go no further, for the door remained closed. The cold hardness of the wood along her backside felt as if it scorched her skin. Behind her, she reached for the latch, searching for its safety.

How could she surrender to this man—a man so familiar, while being an absolute stranger? With her accident, she had lost her identity. Without a history, how could anyone expect her to act as had the former Elizabeth Bennet? How was she to know what was best for her? "What did you...do to me?" she stammered.

"I kissed you." His voice held the desire still simmering between them.

With trembling fingers, she touched her lips. "That was more than a simple kiss." She leaned her head back against the door, realizing, for the first time, her hair had come loose from the chignon, balanced at the nape of her neck. It was as if she, had, literally, unwound before his eyes. "Has this happened previously?" She was so short of breath, she felt as if she had run a long way.

"Do you mean between us? Or ever?" His brows knotted into what could only be called a "scowl."

Despite having only known the man for a matter of weeks, Elizabeth did not enjoy the idea that he had kissed other women. Certainly, he possessed more experience than she, for he had just displayed his prowess in the matter, but the idea he had ever loved another or desired another did not sit well with her. Could her husband have a mistress? Most men of Mr. Darcy's class did. Could she abide with the idea of his sharing himself with another? "Between us," she managed to say.

Tenderly, he caressed her cheek, and Elizabeth made herself not turn away from his touch. Tears pricked at her eyes as the idea of Mr. Darcy and another engaged in a heated kiss formed into a full-blown image claiming her vision. His response did nothing to drive away her sudden jealousy.

"Not so dramatically," he confessed.

For one second, she wished he had lied to her, but she knew such was not of his nature. Biting the inside of her jaw to divert the pain, she nodded her understanding, as her fingers encircled the door's latch. "I should ring for Hannah," she announced on a breathy exhale. Awkwardly turning the latch, she quickly ducked into the room. Without considering her actions, she closed the door in her husband's face.

It was at that moment that her legs collapsed. She sank to her knees. Tears pooled in her eyes, but not from sadness. Rather from loneliness. Although she was not alone in Pemberley House, a feeling of desperation quickly surrounded her.

She did not know how long she had remained as such, rocking herself for comfort, while the tears streamed down her cheeks, but, at length, she realized she could not permit anyone to discover her in such a state. She staggered to her feet and made her way to the bench before the vanity. She glanced to the mirror. The woman staring back at her appeared thoroughly kissed. Pink cheeks. Swollen lips. Hair draped across her shoulders. But something more. Defenseless. Assailable. Exposed. As if her deepest secrets were on display for the world to view, visible to everyone, but her. Her eyes filled with uncertainty as to what to do next.

With fingers still shaking from her encounter with Mr. Darcy, Elizabeth shoved her hair off her cheek. With one kiss, her husband had destroyed any barriers she had constructed.

"This cannot happen," she groused, as she removed the

pins from her hair to pull it into some sense of order. Then she crossed to the wash basin and splashed water onto her face to cool her cheeks and to rinse away any evidence of her tears. She would employ the feminine wiles all women used to protect themselves and then she would tailor herself into Elizabeth Darcy, but she would not surrender to her husband again until she knew the secrets of her past.

Chapter 6

AND SO IT BEGAN. Elizabeth had lain awake for more hours than she cared to consider, waiting for her husband to make an appearance in her quarters, but he had never shown. She had thought after the kiss they had shared, he would have been eager to consummate their agreement. Twice she had made her way to the door separating their chambers and pressed her ear to it, but there was nothing to hear. She was not certain whether Darcy was within, and she was not comfortable entering his quarters without his permission.

After asking directions from a maid, when she reached the morning room, she paused to set her shoulders. She would not allow him more control over her than she had previously ceded to her husband. In spite of her dependence upon his goodness, she could not shake the idea her recovery was in her hands alone. "And if my memory never returns," she whispered, a tearing pain of desolation rushed through her, as if the hand of Fate meant to rip her into twos. How could God place her in such turmoil? How had He forgotten her?

Tears formed in her eyes, and before she could swallow them, they swelled, sending trails streaming down her cheeks.

"May I assist you, Mrs. Darcy?" Mr. Nathan, the butler, said from somewhere off her shoulder.

She made no effort to conceal her tears. "I have changed my mind, Mr. Nathan. I am more exhausted than I first thought. I mean to return to my quarters. Would you ask Cook to send up a tray and offer my apologies for any inconvenience I have caused her?"

"Certainly, ma'am. Should I inform Mr. Darcy of your weariness?"

"That shall not be necessary. I am certain Mr. Darcy's day is full, especially after being from his estate for so long. Later, I will spend time becoming acquainted with my new home."

She was certain her husband could hear her conversation, for she could view him at the head of the table through the crack of the door. He remained very still, as if listening with all his being. Turning toward the stairs, she permitted her tears free rein, as she made her way, once again, to her quarters.

Darcy wished to go after her — to offer her his comfort, but he was at a loss as how best to proceed. After the kiss they had shared the previous evening, he thought to follow her into her quarters and never come out, but something resembling fear had crossed her features, smothering his desire for her.

When Nott had pronounced her injury, Darcy had thought it impossible that *his* Elizabeth could forget their tumultuous courtship. And perhaps that was the problem: She had not forgotten. She had had second thoughts, and she had not held enough nerve to call off their nuptials. Perhaps Mrs. Bennet had convinced Elizabeth to do what was best for the family. After all, when Mr. Bennet passed, Longbourn would go to the Bennet's cousin, Mr. Collins. The welfare of Mrs. Bennet and any unmarried sisters would fall to him and Bingley.

Mayhap it would be best for all if he could shut her out of his mind, but since laying eyes on her, Elizabeth's presence had filled his dreams, as well as his waking hours. Darcy did not think he could tolerate a marriage of convenience with her, but, if her heart belonged to another, he would have no choice. Divorce was a very public affair, and reputations could be ruined forever. Perhaps, if they could settle into a rhythm of life, they could make something comfortable of their days, and his wife could dispense with the charade she practiced.

Darcy glanced about the morning room. How often had he imagined her in this very place? Somehow the familiar suddenly felt drab and uninviting. How could Pemberley so easily alter itself from his adored ancestral home to a yoke about his neck—his punishment for aspiring to the love of a woman who preferred the empty pockets and ready smile of a scoundrel to all the wealth and affection he could offer her?

For two days, he had followed the scent of lavender through the halls of Pemberley, each time hoping for a glimpse of his wife. He cursed himself for being a lofty sentimentalist. Each time he looked in upon her, Elizabeth was in conference with his housekeeper, Mrs. Reynolds. His servant instructed Elizabeth in the running of the estate's manor, something he had repeatedly said he would require of her, and so he did not disturb them. Was not her willingness to accept the duties of the mistress of his estate not a wish he had long cherished? Only yesterday, Mrs. Reynolds had commented when their paths crossed in the upper gallery, "You chose well, Mr. Darcy." It was good to hear his instincts had proven true in that manner. "Your lady is quite knowledgeable in the workings of an estate. If one did not know better, he would assume Mrs. Darcy had graced the halls of Pemberley for years, rather than days."

"Has Mrs. Darcy nothing to learn?" he questioned, almost wishing to find fault, but, instinctively, knowing there was none to find. He had previously argued with himself against her having the knowledge of the duties required to be Pemberley's mistress and lost that battle to the one his heart waged.

"There is always something unexpected, especially with an estate the size of Pemberley, and I am certain Mrs. Darcy will occasionally stumble, but I am more than pleased with her progress and her affability."

Then why was he not likewise pleased? Because he wanted to share in those moments of success and acceptance. He had wanted to be the one who offered her words of praise along with his devotion. He was jealous of not being in a position to look upon her with pride.

※

Elizabeth found she craved her husband's approval, but Mr. Darcy had yet to comment on her efforts to prove herself a worthy mistress of his house. Even when she had rearranged the furniture in the drawing room they shared each evening after supper, he had done nothing more than to lift an eyebrow when he entered the room. His lack of encouragement stung her pride, but she pretended otherwise.

Was such not her wish? To be permitted time to adjust to her role in his life? Then why did she constantly wish to burst into tears of remorse?

The most difficult part of her days had not been the long list of duties Mrs. Reynolds provided her—lists of when to expect the staff to concentrate their efforts on which wing of the house for extensive cleaning—when linens were aired—which merchants were honest and which were not—and lists of Mr. Darcy's tenants, with whom she would be expected to call upon with some regularity, but rather the nearly silent meals.

Each evening, Elizabeth wished to discuss her day with her husband—to seek his advice. While in London, in addition to his aiding her recovery by providing her memories she had lost, he would often read to her, and then they would debate the passage before he continued to the next. He had assured her such was a favorite pastime for her and Mr. Bennet, and he had longed to share such moments with her. She had felt his affection with each of his gestures. Now, all she experienced was her husband's indifference—his tolerating her presence. It appeared Fitzwilliam Darcy could not love in halves, and the idea both pleased and nettled her at the same time.

Elizabeth regretted, literally, placing a door of mistrust between them, but she possessed no means of changing her course beyond welcoming Mr. Darcy into her bed. Unfortunately, her husband thought intimacies was all she required to remember the affection they supposedly shared prior to her accident. What

In Want of a Wife

he did not understand was she did not *fear* him, but rather what would occur if she did not recall their connection? William was so certain their love could resolve all her qualms. Where would their marriage be if she failed him again?

Only yesterday, Elizabeth had been with Mrs. Reynolds when she had asked of a gathering of miniatures upon one of the mantelpieces.

"I thought I had shared these with you and your aunt when you visited Pemberley last August," the lady said with a lift of her brows.

Elizabeth had willed her embarrassment away. Neither she nor Mr. Darcy had shared her memory loss with his Pemberley staff. "Most assuredly, you did," Elizabeth insisted. "I was simply wondering when my husband and the others sat for the miniatures." Without considering the reason behind her reactions, her fingers lovingly traced William's image.

"Mr. Darcy was between his nineteenth and twentieth years. The image is very like him, do you not think?"

Elizabeth's eyes lingered on the miniature. "Perhaps a few more lines about his eyes and mouth," she said wistfully, "but nothing to Mr. Darcy's detriment."

"And the one of Mr. Wickham was done at the same time," Mrs. Reynolds explained.

Elizabeth turned her gaze to the other miniature. *So this was the Mr. Wickham of whom my husband remained so jealous*, she thought. In truth, there was nothing familiar about the man, and that fact bothered her as much as did her impasse with Darcy.

"Mr. Wickham is several months Mr. Darcy's senior, as I suspect you are already aware, as your youngest sister has married the man."

Elizabeth noted the derision in the woman's tone: evidently, Mr. Darcy's dislike for Mr. Wickham was mimicked by those he employed. Despite her instincts warning her not to question Mrs. Reynolds, she asked, "If Mr. Darcy finds Mr. Wickham a less than stellar acquaintance, why does he permit Mr. Wickham's image to be displayed within his home?"

"I suspect Master William does so as an homage to his father. This room was my late master's favorite room, and these miniatures are just as they were when Mr. George Darcy was alive. My late master was very fond of them. The former Mr. Darcy highly respected the late Mr. Wickham. Mr. George Darcy served as godfather to the current Mr. Wickham."

She glanced to her husband silently cutting his meat. She should have taken a tray in her rooms, but she would not permit him to better her with his silence. The clinking of cutlery on china would likely soon drive her to Bedlam, but Elizabeth meant to show him she was made of a sterner disposition than he expected. "When are we to expect the return of Miss Darcy?"

"Week's end. Friday or Saturday. Depending upon the weather." He forked a bite of lamb and chewed it thoroughly.

Watching him from the corner of her eye, she made a silent vow this meal would not pass without conversation. "I will be glad for your sister's company and her guidance. We must consider something of Pemberley's Christmastide celebration, and I would not be so presumptuous as to make plans without her input. I expect your ideas, as well, sir."

Darcy paused, his wine glass halfway to his mouth. "Why would you presume we could celebrate Christmastide this year?"

She did not care for his tone, but Elizabeth had managed to draw his attention away from his meal and his desire to ignore her; therefore, she would count her actions a victory of sorts. "Why would we not, unless you are ashamed of your wife," she accused.

A frown crossed his brow, before he motioned his footmen to withdraw. "Elizabeth, understand me now, I will never know shame at naming you as my wife, but I do not think it best, especially after your injury, to assume such responsibilities. Even a small, intimate celebration at Pemberley will require much of your time. Simply permit Mrs. Reynolds to see to the traditional baskets for the cottagers."

"And what else would you have me do, William? Hide away from your tenants and your neighbors, cherishing the memories of my life before we met?" She tossed her serviette upon the table. "Wait. That cannot be, for I have no memories beyond waking in a bedchamber at Darcy House and my first journey upon a yacht. Those shall not sustain me for long." Everything inside her cautioned her actions were beyond the pale, but she could not prevent the well of tears forming behind her lids. "Do you have any sympathy for how many times each day I wish I could claim one memory all my own?"

Evidently, her words had found their mark. Her husband was immediately upon his feet to reach her. He tugged her upward and into his embrace. "Forgive me," he whispered as he cradled her head against his chest. She clung to him and shed the tears she had fought to hold in check. "I am accustomed to seeing to the needs of everyone in my family circle, but, with you, I am at a loss how to make your life better. I would trade away my wealth and Pemberley to view you whole again. It is a quite sobering reality to have my hands tied where you are concerned. After all is said, you are my love—my future wrapped in this dainty hand." He lifted her fingers to his lips and kissed them tenderly.

She swallowed hard against the panic, always near, rushing to her throat to block her next breath. She caught the back of her husband's head and brought it down where they stood forehead to forehead. "William," she rasped, "we must face the real possibility I may never know anything of my life before my injury, beyond what others share with me."

"I pray each day for a different outcome," he admitted.

"As do I," she replied softly. "However, we must be practical. Even if I held those memories, I would be expected to host several of your acquaintances some time during the Christmas season. I am not an invalid. Other than my lack of personal history, I still possess my faculties about me. I am capable of conversing on a variety of subjects, and if you worry that I might embarrass you—"

"Never," he declared adamantly, as he took a half step back from her.

"Permit me to finish," she insisted. "Even if you unconsciously fear I may experience a bit of embarrassment, you must permit me to move forward with my life as your wife. You and Georgiana may remain close in case I stumble or someone asks a personal question to which I cannot respond. However, I doubt anyone would be so rude to the new mistress of Pemberley." Elizabeth added a soft smile to ward off the frown forming upon her husband's forehead.

After a long moment in which Darcy studied her features, he asked, "This is your wish?"

In spite of his stubbornness, thankfully, her husband was a reasonable man. "It is."

He turned to the chair she had recently vacated and held it for her return. "Then permit us to discuss what is best for both Pemberley and my wife."

Elizabeth swallowed the smile of celebration rushing to her lips. Instead, she nodded her acceptance and sat to their meal.

Later, Mr. Darcy surprised her with his return to her bed. She suspected he had waited for Hannah to leave before a soft knock announced his appearance in her room. "May I join you, Elizabeth?"

For a brief second she wondered if Darcy had misinterpreted the way she had clung to him earlier as an invitation to intimacies, but Elizabeth quickly rejected the idea. Honor flowed through Fitzwilliam Darcy's veins. "I would enjoy your warmth," she said with a blush. "December is turning colder."

He gestured to the fireplace. "Should I put more coal on the fire?"

She shook off the idea before slipping under the bed linens. "I shall be satisfied if you permit me some of your warmth."

Evidently, her words pleased him, for he smiled. "Gladly." He climbed into the bed and settled upon his side before reaching for her. Elizabeth came willingly, permitting him to wrap her into his protective embrace. He sighed heavily. "I have missed you, my love." He gently kissed her temple.

She tugged his hand tighter about her waist. "And I have

missed you, William. Thank you for not abandoning me."

"That would be impossible," he whispered against her shoulder. "A man cannot live without his heart, and you, most assuredly, own mine."

Chapter 7

WITH THINGS BETWEEN THEM easier, the next morning, Elizabeth was pleased to discover her husband at the table when she entered the morning room. An hour earlier, he had kissed her tenderly before he departed their bed, but he had said nothing as to how their day might appear different, after yesterday evening's confrontation. "Good morning," she said as she crossed to the serving table to claim two slices of toast and bacon.

She glanced over her shoulder at him, whose attention remained upon the newspaper he read. A frown claimed her lips as she accepted the chair a footman held for her. "Tea, please," she instructed, before glancing again to her husband. "Good morning, Mr. Darcy," she said with emphasis.

"Good morning," he mumbled, his gaze remaining on his paper.

Elizabeth studied his features, which expressed his disapproval. She might have been one of his servants for all the notice he took of her. Attempting to decide how best to approach him, she spread conserves on the toast before cutting the bread into perfectly proportioned quarters. Then she purposely dropped her knife upon her plate, noticing a slight nod of approval from the footman she knew by the name Jasper, for she recognized him as one of the men who had traveled from London to Derbyshire with her and Mr. Darcy. She made a mental notation to ask Mr. Nathan for the names of the other men who served her husband. She thought it important to claim their loyalty by learning something of each of Mr. Darcy's staff. Elizabeth was certain Hannah would be willing to assist her.

"Are you well?" Mr. Darcy asked, a scowl of rebuke outlining his lips.

"Just requiring my husband's attention," she said pertly, hiding the twitch of amusement ready to claim her lips.

Thankfully, his scowl softened, and a faint smile curled his lips. He leaned nearer. "Have I ever neglected you?" he asked in tones matching hers, indicating he found no complaint with her obvious impertinence.

Elizabeth's insides relaxed. "Not that I recall," she responded with a challenging lift of her eyebrows.

His smile grew wider as she waited for his answer. "I cannot imagine you not remembering such an important detail of our relationship."

"Neither can I." She took a bite of the toast and chewed before she casually remarked. "I was just considering what your father might say to anyone who chose to ignore a pleasant companion by losing himself in a newsprint. From what you have said of the late Mr. Darcy, he would not approve. I am certain your father never ignored your mother."

Her husband placed the paper beside his setting. "I reckon Lady Anne Darcy would have boxed her husband's ears." There was a lightness about his tone that Elizabeth suddenly realized she had longed to hear.

"I am not so aggressive," she observed with a nod that said otherwise. "But on occasion, I have been thought to be outspoken. At least, such is what Mrs. Bingley assured me recently."

His lips slipped into a straight line. "I believe Mrs. Bingley said you have been called *obstinate* and *headstrong* by others."

"Did she? Wherever could she have gotten such an idea?"

He hesitated, obviously considering whether to answer honestly. "I believe your elder sister quoted my Aunt Catherine."

She tilted her head to the side to study him. Surely her husband realized she knew nothing of an aunt named Catherine.

"I cannot imagine what offense I offered your aunt to term me immovable," she remarked lamely.

"Lady Catherine found it unfathomable that you dared to set your sights upon her most estimable nephew." A hint of amusement had remained in his tone.

Elizabeth hid the smile rushing to her lips. He had not placed her in an awkward position before his servants. Keeping his tone light, her husband had provided her information others would expect her to know. "I believe you set your sights upon me, rather than the other way around, sir."

William reached across the table to squeeze the back of her hand. "I did at that, Mrs. Darcy, and I count each day with you fortunate."

She purposely changed the topic, knowing she must learn more of her husband's aunt and what had occurred between them, but now was not the time. "What, pray tell, so occupied your mind in the papers?"

"I was reading something of the changes coming to Parliament after the general election last month." At least her injury had not robbed her of all her mental faculties: she knew something of politics and history and the like. Certainly, nothing to compare with her husband, who seemed to be able to converse upon a wide variety of topics with ease. She nodded for him to continue. "I am excessively interested in how this latest general election will change the face of Parliament. More than a quarter of the seats were contested. The issue of Catholic relief is no longer something to be set aside. It has made itself known. The most spectacular contest proved to be as near as Liverpool, which means soon it will be on Derbyshire's doorstep. Parliamentary reform and the prospect of war with the United States appears imminent."

"Another war? We have not found peace yet with Napoleon." The idea made her uneasy.

Her husband matched her frown with one of his own. "I worry for my cousin," he admitted. "Colonel Fitzwilliam spoke recently of rumors of his being sent to the Canadian front. And now, the political picture appears in upheaval."

"How so?" she asked.

"The Tory candidates, George Canning and Isaac Gascoyne, defeated their Whig counterparts Henry Brougham and Thomas Creevey. Several more Whigs failed to find a seat or were defeated, including William Lamb, Richard Sheridan, Francis Horner, George Tierney, and Sir Samuel Romilly."

"It sounds as if many who earned seats will have no parliamentary experience," she observed. "Will that play fair or foul for England?"

"It is hard to say," he admitted. "Fresh ideas are never ill; yet, the loss of experience and parliamentary influence will affect many rural areas."

"And Pemberley?" she asked.

"All estates have seen the loss of cottagers to the textile centers, but Pemberley has faired better than many estates in the area; yet, we are not completely immune to the loss of long-time tenants. I am always looking for ways to improve yields and conditions for those who call Pemberley home."

Something in the manner in which her husband spoke had her listening with all her heart. He was so strong, but Pemberley and the responsibilities he held to it were his Achilles' heel: Where he feared failure. Elizabeth ventured, "Would you accept my suggestions?"

He interlaced their fingers and looked upon her with gratefulness. "I have always believed much of my father's success as Pemberley's master rested in the stroke of my mother's hands across his soul." He lifted their joined hands to kiss her knuckles. "It would please me for you to take an interest in Pemberley's future. Such has been my greatest desire since I first laid eyes upon you."

After breakfast, she and her husband adjourned to his study. There he took time to explain something of his Matlock relations: his aunt and uncle, the Earl and Countess of Matlock, his cousins, Roland, Lord Lindale, Matlock's heir, and the younger son and Darcy's best friend, Edward, a colonel in His Majesty's army, the one over whom her husband fretted for his safety, a cousin with whom she supposedly held an acquaintance. That was followed by a brief introduction to Lady Catherine de Bourgh, Darcy's aunt, and the woman who had disapproved of Elizabeth as Darcy's wife. "My aunt wished me to marry my Cousin Anne," he explained. "Such was never the wish of either Anne or me, but Lady Catherine is not one who changes her mind easily, and so we 'danced' about the subject for years. She claimed the marriage between cousins was the wish of my mother, but Lady Anne Darcy never spoke of such to either me or my father before she passed. However, Lady Catherine is not the type to believe her views unreasonable." He leaned down to kiss her gently. "Unfortunately, I have not the time to share the whole tale with you at this moment, for I have a meeting with my steward regarding the new mill I plan to aid my cottagers with their corn. Yet, I make you this promise to explain it all to your satisfaction this evening after supper."

"There you are, Mrs. Darcy." Elizabeth looked up to find Mrs. Reynolds waiting patiently by the open library door.

"Did we have an appointment?" she asked the lady.

"No, ma'am. I was planning to go into Lambton and place the order for the items we discussed for the baskets for the cottagers and for our Christmas supper. I thought perhaps you might wish to accompany me. I know you stayed at The Rose and Crown last August, but you were Miss Bennet then. It would do you well to be seen as Pemberley's mistress before the various merchants."

"I would enjoy time away from the house," she began tentatively. "With Miss Darcy's absence and Mr. Darcy's tending to the estate—" She did not finish her thoughts. It was not appropriate, as Darcy's wife, to express her fears aloud.

"Pemberley is quite large and can be overwhelmingly empty," Mrs. Reynolds sympathized.

Elizabeth experienced a shiver of panic skittering down

her spine. How could she hope to manage without Mr. Darcy by her side? "If you hold no objections, I would ask Hannah to join us. I am certain my lady's maid will enjoy a few minutes with her uncle's family at the inn, and while you tend to the household business, she can go with me about the village. It would not do for Mr. Darcy's wife to be seen as not practicing propriety."

Mrs. Reynolds judiciously agreed. "I shall send Hannah to assist you to dress and also ask Mr. Nathan to order the small coach. Say thirty minutes for our departure?"

"Excellent. I appreciate your considering my transition into the role of mistress of Pemberley."

Mrs. Reynolds had made the introductions in the first two shops they frequented, but when the good lady was called upon to provide her expertise to the baker's wife, Elizabeth seized the opportunity to make her own way. "Come, Hannah, we should use our time wisely." To Mr. Higgenbotham she said, "Please tell Mrs. Reynolds I shall meet her at the inn in half an hour. I mean to look over the items at the mercantile to choose a fairing for Miss Darcy."

The baker bowed respectfully. "Certainly, Mrs. Darcy. Mrs. Higgenbotham and I are pleased you've come to Pemberley."

With that, Elizabeth led the way to the mercantile two doors down. Entering the shop, she waited patiently for the shop owner to complete his transaction. With the exit of the previous customer, the man nodded to Hannah, before saying, "How might I be of assistance, ma'am?"

Elizabeth noted Hannah thought to make the introduction, but she stayed her maid with a hand upon Hannah's sleeve. "I am Mrs. Darcy," she announced in a voice loud enough for the shop's employees and two other customers, lingering near the rear of the shop, to hear. "I came today to have your acquaintance, as well as to purchase a small gift for my sister, Miss Darcy." Knowing first impressions were sometimes lasting ones, she held her head high and her posture perfect. Elizabeth meant not to disappoint her husband; he already had enough to contend with regarding her memory loss. The village depended upon Pemberley, and as the estate's mistress, what she did—how she acted in this moment—without her husband standing at her side—would set the tone for the remainder of her days.

"Certainly, ma'am." The man bowed again. "We had heard that Mr. Darcy meant to marry and were glad to have your husband see to Pemberley's future." Elizabeth swallowed the flush of embarrassment racing to her cheeks. The shopkeeper spoke of her delivering an heir for Pemberley, but, first, she must welcome her husband into her bed under different circumstances. "I am Mr. Andrews, and the young man behind you be my son Haston. I fear Mrs. Andrews is currently away tending our daughter Faith, during her lying in. Mrs. Andrews will be sorry to have missed taking your acquaintance."

Elizabeth glanced toward a table at the side of the store. "Earlier, through your window, I noted a small crystal figurine on the table. I thought Miss Darcy would take a liking to it."

Mr. Andrews came from behind the counter. "I know just the one you mean. Miss Darcy does love her music. I have heard her play on two separate occasions. She be quite *accomplished*."

The word struck a chord in Elizabeth. There was something important wrapped about it, but she could not name the event. Perhaps if she should ask Darcy of its significance, he would know if it had something to do with their courtship. Then again, mayhap she should keep her own counsel for the time being. *What if Mr. Wickham spoke of my accomplishments, rather than Mr. Darcy?* She did not want another round of jealousy displayed by her husband, especially as they were on better ground, at last. "Most assuredly," she murmured as Mr. Andrews handed her the only crystal figurine from the table display of china.

Elizabeth accepted it from the man and examined it. "What do you think, Hannah? Will Miss Darcy like it?"

Hannah blushed from the recognition, but the maid answered in honest tones. "When I served Miss Darcy, she spent equal time on both the harp and the pianoforte. The late Mrs. Darcy excelled on the harp. The harp would be an excellent reminder of Lady Anne's love for her daughter."

"Such is why I asked your opinion," Elizabeth said evenly, having realized she had placed Hannah in an awkward position. The information Hannah shared, Elizabeth had no means of knowing until this moment. She turned to focus upon the small crystal harp and its whispers of glass strings. In her opinion, anyone would appreciate the delicate touches of detail. "I believe this will serve Miss Darcy well." She returned the item to Mr. Andrews's hand. "If you will wrap it carefully, I will send Mr. Jasper to retrieve it." She followed Mr. Andrews to the counter and opened her reticule.

"I can place the item on Mr. Darcy's account, ma'am."

Elizabeth shook her head in the negative. "I wish the item to be a gift from me, not Mr. Darcy."

Hannah remarked softly, so as the others would not hear. "You might use your pin money, ma'am. I am certain the master has provided you an adequate account."

Elizabeth nodded her gratitude before instructing Mr. Andrews. "You will open an account specifically under my name. If I choose items for the household, the bill will be sent to Mr. Darcy's attention. Special items such as this fairing for Miss Darcy, we shall place on my account."

"Most assuredly, Mrs. Darcy," the shopkeeper said with a smile. She had no doubt the man would ask Darcy if he minded her keeping separate account books from his, and she prayed her husband would understand her need to control her future and not assume she kept something secreted away from him.

Things settled, she turned to the maid. "Come, Hannah. I promised to meet Mrs. Reynolds at the inn, and I wish you a few moments to spend with your family before we return to Pemberley. It has been nearly two months since you last saw them." Elizabeth nodded to the shopkeeper. "Thank you, Mr. Andrews. I am certain we shall see each other soon."

Outside once again, Elizabeth accepted Hannah's steady hand as they crossed the street, which was still muddy from the recent rains. "I did not consider my pin money. Thank you for the reminder."

"My pleasure, ma'am."

They entered the inn to be greeted by Hannah's uncle. "If I had known you'd call upon us today, Mrs. Darcy, I would have set aside a couple of those raisin-filled cakes of which you were so fond when last you were here."

"I shall be happy with a cup of tea and a warm fire, Mr. Crownley."

"Right away, ma'am." He held a chair for Elizabeth before scurrying away to order her tea.

"Go." Elizabeth ordered Hannah, pointing toward the kitchen. "I shall be well. Jasper waits by the door. No one shall accost me."

"I shall have one cup of tea and then return," Hannah assured.

"Have two," Elizabeth instructed.

Darcy handed off his coat and gloves to Mr. Nathan. "Do you know where my wife might be?" He could not forget the teasing tone his wife had employed this morning. Darcy prayed such was a prelude to the return of Elizabeth's memory.

"Mrs. Darcy is out, sir," Mr. Nathan announced.

"Out?"

"Yes, sir. The mistress accompanied Mrs. Reynolds into Lambton. They were to see to the items for the tenants' baskets. I believe Mrs. Reynolds meant to introduce Mrs. Darcy to several of the shopkeepers."

Darcy knew Mrs. Reynolds meant well, but with Elizabeth's memory loss, he did not wish for his wife to encounter too many new acquaintances at once, and he knew the good people of Lambton would each wish to claim her attention. Such was his objection to their hosting an entertainment. They had no way of knowing whether or not doing so would cause her harm, and Darcy would err on the side of her safety. "Ask Mr. Fergus to bring my horse back around. I believe I will join my lady in the village. Perhaps we can share tea at the inn."

"Good day, Mrs. Darcy."

Elizabeth looked up to view a remarkably lovely woman standing nearby. The arresting quality of the lady's appearance had Elizabeth silently comparing herself to the woman and finding herself wanting. The lady possessed a delicate bone structure and deep blue-violet eyes framed by dark lashes.

"Good day," Elizabeth responded. She waited for the woman to say more, but the lady did not appear inclined to make her curtsey and move along.

Thankfully, Mr. Crownley appeared with the teapot, cup and a plate of cakes. "Here ye be, Mrs. Darcy."

Elizabeth shot a quick glance to the woman who still stood nearby. "Thank you, sir."

The man frowned when he noted the woman lurking so closely, and Elizabeth wondered at the innkeeper's reaction. "Do you require something, Mrs. Avendell?" There was a note of disapproval in his tone.

"Tea," the woman said with a lift of her chin.

"You will sit over by the window," Mr. Crownley ordered. "Mrs. Darcy does not require the likes of you disturbing her."

The woman glared at the innkeeper, but she did as he said.

"I'll send Hannah out to sit with you, ma'am." Mr. Crownley's scowl deepened as he shot another glance to the woman. "I be apologizing for the likes of some of my fellow shopkeepers in Lambton. Some people do not know their place. Hannah will be right out. I shan't have you left defenseless."

Elizabeth did not understand what the woman had done to upset the innkeeper, but she permitted the man his censure. Perhaps Hannah could provide an explanation.

Chapter 8

WHEN HANNAH JOINED ELIZABETH, she said softly, "I am grieved to pull you away from your family so soon."

"It is of no consequence, ma'am. My half day be two days removed. I can call upon my uncle then. Besides, the new Mrs. Crownley and her daughters are less than welcoming to my side of the family."

Elizabeth glanced to the woman by the window. Mr. Crownley placed the teapot and cup before the woman with a prominent *thunk* against the table. "How did the lady know my name?" she whispered.

Hannah's gaze fell upon the woman. "The lady's late husband owned the local bookstore and tobacco shop. You called upon the bookstore several times when you were visiting the area last August." She leaned closer to say. "I imagine my uncle has bragged of my position in service to you and of how Mr. Darcy brought his sister to this very inn to take your acquaintance. The people in Lambton who depend on Pemberley are interested in the family, and they took note of Mr. Darcy's attentions to you. Even after you left so quickly, there was great speculation that Mr. Darcy would follow you. When it was reported that, despite having houseguests, the master had unexpectedly gone to London 'on business,' most of the village speculated on his doing so in order to win your hand."

Elizabeth did not know all of the tale Hannah related, but

it would not do to question her maid on it when others might overhear. Instead, she slid the cake plate closer to Hannah and motioned for her trusted servant to enjoy one of the fruit-filled concoctions.

"I should not," Hannah protested.

Elizabeth smiled upon the young woman who was truly a buoy in this messy business of her memory loss. "You should not follow your mistress's orders?" she teased.

Hannah blushed, but she did not turn subservient in her posture, a personality trait which Elizabeth appreciated. Although they were of different stations, Hannah had become a trusted friend and confidante. The maid smiled before teasingly saying, "I must have also suffered a recent injury to my head, for I do not recall my mistress issuing an order."

"A suggestion then," Elizabeth said with a wide smile.

"You are too generous, Mrs. Darcy," Hannah insisted. "And I have already broken with propriety by sharing a table with you."

"Oh, but you must," Elizabeth countered. "I cannot possibly think to partake of either tea or cakes while you have none. You would not wish to give the impression that I think myself too lofty to share a simple meal with the best lady's maid a woman could claim."

Hannah laughed softly. "First, serving you is easy compared to the stories I have heard from the footmen who accompany Mr. Darcy. They tell grand tales of some of the women the master encounters, or I should say 'encountered,' before he was married." Hannah paused to study Elizabeth briefly. "I am thankful each day for your kindness to me, ma'am." Then with another chuckle, the maid declared, "Mr. Darcy has no idea how much chaos you will bring to his life."

Elizabeth returned the maid's smile. "Do you think *chaos* will please my husband?"

"The master's well-ordered world has become too staid. You shall be a refreshing wind to drive away Mr. Darcy's decorous plan for his life."

In Want of a Wife

Elizabeth squeezed the back of Hannah's hand. "I needed to hear someone declare me more than another duty for which my husband is responsible."

"You should never think yourself less than the love of Mr. Darcy's life," Hannah declared. "The master was quite distraught when he thought to lose you."

Elizabeth fought the tears rushing to her eyes. She wished Hannah's words true, but she feared Mr. Darcy would soon tire of her unless she agreed to become his wife again in all ways possible.

When Mrs. Avendell rose to depart, Elizabeth's curiosity returned. "Why does Mr. Crownley disapprove of the lady?"

Hannah lowered her voice further. "Although the woman wears gowns to disguise her condition, it is rumored that Mrs. Avendell is with child."

"And that is a problem because—" Elizabeth whispered.

"Because Mr. Avendell has been dead for nearly two years."

Darcy dismounted before the inn, tossing Diablo's reins and a coin to the groom rushing out to meet him. He spotted his small coach at the far side of the inn yard. "Are my wife and housekeeper about?" he asked the young man.

"Kint say, sir, but yer man Jasper be inside."

Darcy nodded his thanks and started for the inn. However, the appearance of Mrs. Avendell brought him up short. He had not seen the lady in more months than he could name. He had quietly ceased his dealings with the woman after his return to Pemberley following Elizabeth's first rejection of his hand in marriage, for Mrs. Avendell had made it known by the occasional brush of her hand over his and knowing glances that she would be happy to receive his attentions. As he had been miserable beyond speaking, not able to consider anyone but Elizabeth Bennet at his side, he had simply refused to patronize the lady's shop again.

He had been home for nearly three months when he eventually encountered the woman on one of the trails marking the outskirts of Pemberley proper. It was only afterwards that he wondered why he had not questioned her presence on his property.

In truth, if he had had his wits about him on that day, he would have turned his horse upon a different path, but, for several days, he had drowned his sorrows of never knowing the woman for whom he yearned in more brandy than he had ever consumed previously. Therefore, he had dismounted and greeted the woman, a mistake upon a grand scale.

Charlotte Fordham had been a favorite of all the local males of a certain age when Darcy was still in his university years. Every fellow for miles around thought to court her, but her father had accepted Jacob Avendell's proposal for Miss Fordham. Avendell was some twenty years Miss Fordham's senior, but the woman had appeared willing to marry a man who was rich by village standards.

George Darcy had never permitted his son to be one of those who had vied for Miss Fordham's favors at the local assemblies. In fact, Darcy had not spoken to the girl more than a dozen times before she married the owner of the local bookseller. After that, they regularly spoke, for both his father and Darcy often called at the shop. Even then, their conversations had dwelt on a particular book being in stock or the need to have it ordered.

Therefore, being deep in his cups and heartsick, the day he encountered Mrs. Avendell on the trail, Darcy quickly felt drawn by her flirtations—the arts and allurements he had judiciously ignored for years, just as he pretended to be ignorant of the number of society mamas who placed their daughters before him. As foolish as it would sound to admit aloud, he wished to banish the ghost of Elizabeth Bennet and her *"I had not known you a month before I felt that you were the last man in the world whom I could ever be prevailed upon to marry."* He wanted to prove Miss Elizabeth's admonishments unfounded, and so he had walked with Mrs. Avendell and had accepted the lady's attention and her kisses until the voice of his father's warning rang in his head: *Darcy, you cannot act without honor.*

Afterwards, Darcy had accepted Bingley's invitation to join him in Town. Later, Bingley and his sisters and Georgiana had returned to Pemberley with Darcy to celebrate Georgiana's birthday in early August. It was then that he had come across Elizabeth Bennet and the Gardiners at Pemberley. She appeared to no longer disdain him, and so he had moved heaven and earth to reclaim her. If he had continued with a dalliance with Mrs. Avendell, everything he had planned for his life with Elizabeth would have been placed in jeopardy, for he knew his wife was not of the nature to turn her pretty head while he spread his seed elsewhere. Moreover, he was not of the nature to lust after any woman except Elizabeth Darcy.

"Mr. Darcy." The woman offered him a brief curtsey.

"Mrs. Avendell." He nodded his acknowledgement and started around her, but she caught his sleeve to stay him.

Darcy glared at her. "You forget yourself, madam."

She quickly withdrew her hand, but not her eyes. "There was a time—" she began.

"There was one time," he corrected. "I was not myself that day, and nothing of significance occurred between us."

"Something occurred," she argued, "or else you would still frequent my shop."

"There is nothing at Avendell's which interests me," he pronounced in cold tones. "Now, you will pardon me. My wife awaits within."

⁂

Elizabeth's eyes had naturally followed Mrs. Avendell's exit, and she wished she had not permitted them to do so, for the lady stopped to speak to a gentleman, and even without seeing his face, Elizabeth knew the man was Mr. Darcy. She would recognize the tilt of her husband's shoulders anywhere. There could be no other gentleman in the area who held himself to such high standards.

As Hannah shared the rumors of Mrs. Avendell's deepest secrets, Elizabeth watched as the woman's expression softened when she looked upon Mr. Darcy. Elizabeth wished she could view whether her husband returned Mrs. Avendell's interest, but perhaps it was best that she did not know. Although her time with Mr. Darcy had been short, he had claimed a place in her heart, and she would be sore to know his words of devotion to her proved to be false. Moreover, the scene left the taste of jealousy in her mouth, and, for the first time, she knew something of her husband's mania.

As the door to the inn opened, Elizabeth withdrew her eyes from the retreating form of Mrs. Avendell in time to place a smile of welcome upon her lips to greet her husband.

"William," she said as he approached. "How very kind of you to follow me into Lambton."

"I returned to the manor so we might have tea together," he said as he placed his coat and hat upon an empty chair.

"If I had known you meant to return for the midday meal, I would have remained at the estate."

"No censure intended, my love," he said with confidence. "We can share something here, and then I will escort you back to Pemberley."

Hannah had risen when Darcy approached the table, and so she made her curtsey. "I shall ask my uncle to see to your needs." To Elizabeth she said, "With your permission, ma'am, I will retrieve Miss Darcy's gift from Mr. Higgenbotham and then see if Mrs. Reynolds requires my assistance."

Elizabeth nodded her agreement. "Take Jasper with you. I imagine Mrs. Reynolds will have her arms full."

"Yes, ma'am."

"A gift for Georgiana?" he questioned as Hannah made her exit.

"Through the window, I saw it on a table in Mr. Higgenbotham's establishment. It is a small crystal harp. Do you think she will like it?"

Her husband shot her an impish grin. "I imagine Georgiana would cherish any fairing she receives from her new sister. The fact such gift is a harp will double her pleasure."

"Hannah said your mother held a reputation as being

quite proficient on the harp."

"She was. Lady Anne loved her music. She won my father's heart with her beauty and her mesmerizing technique on the instrument. George Darcy regularly claimed Lady Anne could make the harp's strings sing."

"I am sorry I never had the opportunity to take her acquaintance," Elizabeth declared in honest tones.

"As am I," William admitted. "I have no doubt she would have adored you."

"It sounds as if your parents were opposing stars," she observed.

Her husband attempted to bury his grin, but he was not successful. "They were a formidable pair. Such is my wish for us. I imagine we can be equally redoubtable."

Mr. Crownley's appearance interrupted their discussion. Elizabeth took the time to pour Darcy his tea, while her husband placed an order for their meal. When they were alone again, she ventured, "I noted you spoke to Mrs. Avendell on your way in."

"How are you aware of the woman?" he asked suspiciously.

"Nothing to do with my memory loss," she whispered.

They were the only ones in the inn's common area.

"I was not questioning your memory," he assured. "Only how you came to claim Mrs. Avendell's acquaintance."

Hearing voices from the direction of the kitchen, Elizabeth glanced about to make certain no one could overhear their conversation. "The lady meant to introduce herself."

"The practiced cheek, you say. How dare she!" Fury marked her husband's features.

Elizabeth rushed to say. "Mr. Crownley stepped in and sent Mrs. Avendell upon her way." She attempted to assuage her husband's concerns. "Hannah seemed to think I had spoken to the woman previously when I was here in August. Perhaps, Mrs. Avendell only meant to extend her regards for our marriage." Elizabeth had no reason to think her words held the truth. She had certainly not approved of the manner in which the woman had looked upon Mr. Darcy.

"Mrs. Avendell should know better," her husband said stubbornly. "As my wife, it is your prerogative to seek her acquaintance, not contrariwise."

Innocently, Elizabeth asked, "Did Mrs. Avendell ask of me when you spoke moments ago?"

An ungovernable annoyance crossed her husband's features before he brought his expression under control. What did Mr. Darcy disguise regarding his relationship with Mrs. Avendell? "The lady simply commented on how the village was glad for my return to Pemberley before Christmastide."

"Are you not customarily present at Pemberley during this time of year?" she inquired. "I thought it odd when Mrs. Reynolds spoke of the absence of preparations for the house in previous years, going so far as to say she was not certain whether the remains of the last Yule log to be burned in the great hall was still available, but I assumed because Miss Darcy was too young to serve as your hostess that you had chosen not to entertain."

"Not exactly. Georgiana is still a bit young, and, as I assume you have learned, my sister is excessively shy; however, for the last five years, since the death of our father, Georgiana and I have found it difficult to enjoy the festivities. Our father took ill over Christmastide, with a steady decline until his passing in February."

"Why did you not say something? I feel such a fool for arguing with you over the preparations Mrs. Reynolds and I made," Elizabeth protested.

"How could I object? I specifically brought you to Pemberley to bring new life to the estate and my father's prized heritage. My only concern regarding the plans you made was for your health. You are what is important. A renewal of the traditions my family once held dear would mean nothing to either Georgiana or me if you were too ill to stand with us during the festivities." He searched her face for understanding, and so, she nodded her encouragement to continue. "I realize you do not recall the conversation before our marriage where I spoke of my hopes for us at Pemberley."

Beneath the table, she slid her hand into his. "If it would not be too tiresome, would you repeat it for my benefit?"

A tender smile crossed her husband's lips. "I explained how it was my belief that my father waited until I reached my majority and assumed control of parts of Pemberley's operations before George Darcy permitted his decline. I have often thought he would have followed Lady Anne into death if my mother had not exacted a promise from him on her death bed to see me well-settled in the role of Pemberley's master and Georgiana's guardian before he joined her. I turned three and twenty in September, having assumed much of the running of the estate by that time. By December, all the legal papers were in place, and between us, father and I had a plan for investments, Georgiana's presentation, and the advancement of Pemberley's future."

"How was I part of that plan?" she asked innocently.

His thumb made calming circles on the back of her gloved hand. "At father's passing, there was no plan for Elizabeth Bennet to rob me of my customary good sense."

"Good sense?" she charged.

"In our past, you called my *caution* more vile names, but you learned to overlook my faults and admire my merits," he teased.

Elizabeth good-naturedly rolled her eyes. "I pray daily for a return of my memory so I might prove you have distorted the truth of our coming together."

He chuckled and brought the back of her hand to his lips. "You led me through a merry dance, my lady."

"Until I captured you or did you capture me?" she challenged.

He leaned closer to whisper, "Until you took pity on my sorry state."

She leaned close enough to place a gentle kiss on his temple. "Our finding each other is by far my favorite memory of those you have shared, sir."

"I am pleased," he said softly. "And, although I did not know your name at the time, as to your part in the plan George

Darcy and I created for Pemberley, I did know exactly the role you would play in Pemberley's great legacy. Pemberley, Georgiana, and I require a woman to carry the essence of Lady Anne Darcy forward, while placing her own mark on each of us. 'Our family,' my father was fond of saying, 'always comes first. Pemberley will only survive when our family is strong.' He once told me of these vines that grow in both the Americas and Africa. They are called *Entada gigas*, but more commonly known as lianas. When my father would talk of a strong family, I would envision the lianas. First, like most vines, lianas have their roots in the ground, but their roots are quite thick and knotted, reminding me of our ancestors holding us up, anchoring us, and permitting the vine to grow upward into the canopy of the trees, secured at both ends. A person might sway back and forth on it, but unless he lets go, he will not fall. If someone dares to yank on it — to try and bring the liana vine down, it will rain down a multitude of bugs and nasty business upon the person, driving him away, while leaving the liana intact. More importantly, because the lianas sway, those of us climbing to reach its greatness can swing horizontally from one liana to another to reach our next plateau." He looked at her sheepishly and shrugged, embarrassed by all he said.

Yet, Elizabeth recognized what her husband said as symbolically true. She caressed his chin line and whispered, "I am ready to climb a liana with you, William."

He leaned forward to kiss her forehead before sighing. "My father was correct, perhaps not about the lianas, but about what a man required to know his destiny. You are the missing link in the Darcy family chain. Through you, we will embrace the beauty of life. Upon your sweet lips I taste the promise of the smile of our children and the strength of family. In your eyes, I view the love of a mother and the joy of a father. Family is a special gift to be treasured. You once told my aunt you had not studied the great painters, but it is by your hand that the Darcy family and Pemberley will become a masterpiece for all to admire."

Chapter 9

ALTHOUGH HER HUSBAND'S WORDS had touched her heart, Elizabeth could not forget the look of longing Mrs. Avendell presented Mr. Darcy, and so she questioned both Hannah and Mrs. Reynolds regarding the woman. As expected, Hannah was more forthcoming than was the Pemberley housekeeper; yet, neither provided any information that would prove a connection between Darcy and the lady, and after two days of privately fretting over something that evidently had no basis, she made herself set her qualms aside. Surely a man as handsome and as wealthy as her husband regularly garnered unwanted attention.

"I found you at last."

Elizabeth looked up to discover her husband leisurely leaning against the doorway, his shoulder propped against the frame, arms crossed over his chest, and his legs crossed at the ankles. She realized he had been studying her, as she so often studied him—as she had for more than a hundred times since she woke at Darcy House nearly a month prior. His was not a countenance one easily forgot, but somehow she had, which never ceased to amaze her or irritate him tremendously. Thick brown hair outlined his face. High cheek bones. Expressive eyes when he permitted them to be so. His was a face to quell the opposition of powerful men and slay the protests of even the most fastidious of women—as she, according to everyone, had once been.

"I was not aware you sought me out, sir."

"It would be a cold day in the Devil's realm when I would not search for you, Elizabeth," he said in honest tones as he stood straight. "I thought while the temperature and the elements permitted, we might walk the grounds together."

"Have you not obligations to the estate?" she inquired as she stood. Although she spoke of his returning to his duties to Pemberley, the idea of their spending time together greatly tempted her.

"Not an hour passes that I am not petitioned for my opinion on some facet of the workings of Pemberley. However, I have disciplined myself of late to think beyond seed yields and the cost of wool. This estate will not crumble into dust if I choose also to nourish my relationship with my wife." He exhaled sharply. "I enjoyed our tea at the inn, and I would prefer to continue to woo my lovely wife."

"Just today?" she asked in hesitation, for Mr. Darcy was doing as she had asked. He was offering to court her.

"I hope it will become the mark of our marriage," he responded in what sounded of sincerity.

She answered in equal honesty. "As would I, but I pray it never becomes another duty for you."

"And I would express my like prayers that your affections will continue until we take our last breath."

She smiled at him. "A morbidly pleasant concept."

"I suppose in some opinions it is so." His smile widened.

"Permit me to claim my pelisse." She started for her dressing room.

"The one your very generous husband purchased for you?" His tone was light.

She grinned back. "He is an exceptional husband, and I am blessed to have him in my life."

They viewed the conservatory first, and she was surprised to discover how many plants his staff oversaw. Beyond the customary exotic flowers and fruits, there were also "experiments" where the gardeners crossed two varieties of existing plants to create a stronger one with a higher yield. Her husband was obviously a forward-thinking man—a man with a great vision, and, briefly, Elizabeth wondered how she could intricately become a part of his world.

Finally, they struck out on the lower paths of the estate's natural trails. Despite the weak sun, it felt wonderful to be outside and on the arm of her husband. "This is magnificent, William."

"You approve?"

"Who would not?"

"But your approval is not so freely given and, therefore, doubly appreciated."

"You make me sound quite contrary, sir," she protested, wondering once again how he could ever have taken a liking to her if she always set herself against him.

"Adorably so," he said as he patted the back of her hand as if to calm her worries.

At length, they entered a beautiful walk by the side of the lake. In her humble opinion, every step brought forward a nobler fall of ground or a finer reach of the woods they were approaching.

"The entrance hall and the lower rooms and the east wing were built in the late 1600s," he explained when they paused to look back at Pemberley House from their vantage point, "but there was a fire in 1720 that required the family wing to be rebuilt. Each generation since has added to the original manor, thankfully, keeping the integrity of the architecture."

She rose up on her toes for a better view of the manor house. "It is amazing that the additional wings are compatible to the original."

"We have my great-grandfather to thank for the current appearance of our home. Robert Darcy commissioned a brick making facility to fashion the necessary stones to repair the buttress and had the whole house repainted. Since then, we employ workers to maintain the necessary repairs inside and out."

She asked if such included the painting of drawing rooms

and the sort, and he confirmed that if she wished to make any changes, workers were at her disposal. Her husband did not even question if she wished to alter any of the rooms, just simply told her she was free to do so. No questions. Simply trust. The idea pleased her.

Eventually, they entered the wood and ascended some of the higher ground.

"The vistas are breathtaking," she remarked as she studied a charming view of the valley stretching out to the west. "How far is it about the whole park?"

"It is beyond a simple walk, even for one who is known by her family to be a great walker," he said with a triumphant smile. "It is a bit over ten miles."

"Perhaps another day," she responded with an impish grin.

Silently, but contentedly, they assumed the accustomed circuit, which brought them again, after some time, in a descent among hanging woods, to the edge of the water, and at one of its narrowest parts. They crossed it by a simple bridge, in character with the general air of the scene. At this point, the valley contracted into a glen, allowing room only for the stream and a narrow walk amid the rough coppice-wood which bordered it.

"This is where I joined your party when you and the Gardiners visited Pemberley last August," he explained when they came to a standstill.

"Such was an important part of our coming together?" she asked.

"You had adamantly refused me in April. At first, I ranted and raved against the injustice of presenting my heart to a woman who could not appreciate a man of my good standing in the world," he declared simply.

"I am sorry I brought grief to your heart," she whispered.

He cupped her chin with his fingers. "I was the one who erred. My stubborn pride had me thinking my opinions absolute. I deserved your rebukes."

Stunned, she sat upon a nearby bench. "How could you

think to continue to love me?"

"It was a bit difficult to realize how repulsed you were by me. You called your opinion of me an 'immovable dislike,' going so far as to say I could not have made you the offer of my hand in any possible way that would have tempted you to accept me."

"Oh my," she murmured, again wondering about the nature of the way she had treated him and what her doing so said of her personality and his absolute forgiveness. It also spoke to his jealousy and her husband's harried need to be loved. "I was that cruel to you? How could you think to pardon my earlier accusations?"

"We both erred." He caught her hand in his. "My abominable pride had me acting without forethought. Thankfully, you finally realized, despite my missteps, I had not acted without principles. Your being with your relations at Pemberley allowed us to come to a better understanding."

༺༻

Their walk the previous day had proven to be the preamble for a delightful evening. They had played a highly contested game of chess before curling up together upon a settee before a fire. He read poems by Cowper to her, for she had once told him Cowper was a favorite. If they could have ended the evening in his bed, he would have termed their day perfection. Even though she chose for them to sleep in her bed instead of enjoying intimacies in his, he felt they had made progress. She no longer avoided his touch.

Unfortunately, at breakfast the next morning, Mr. Nathan delivered an express from Mr. Cowan.

"What is it, William?" she asked.

Darcy's frown deepened. "It appears I must leave for Manchester for a few days." Cowan's message said the former Runner had trailed Mr. Wickham to the city west of Derbyshire. The investigator had no idea why Darcy's former friend had departed London for the manufacturing city.

"But Miss Darcy arrives tomorrow," his wife argued.

He looked upon her lovely features and wondered if this

"madness" would ever know an end. Yesterday had held hope for the future for which he had gambled his heritage. Sadly, every time he thought to know peace, the image of George Wickham darting away from the scene of Elizabeth's accident had Darcy wishing to roar at the injustice.

"It cannot be helped," he said as he shoved the note from Cowan into his pocket. "I should not be absent from Pemberley for more than four days, five at the longest."

"Cannot your steward see to the matter?" she pleaded.

"The issue is of a personal nature," he countered.

He attempted to school his features, but he had failed, for his wife's frown deepened. "Is it something to do with my accident?" she whispered.

Despite the feeling of doom filling his chest, he assured, "Absolutely not. Just a tenuous negotiation that requires my presence. I promise not to tarry any longer than necessary." He made himself smile upon her. "My absence will provide you and Georgiana the opportunity to plan your Christmastide celebrations."

"I shall miss you," she said in softness. "Pray, return safely to us. To me."

Elizabeth woke with a start, the pain in her head had returned with a vengeance, and she squeezed her eyes tight shut. However, the dream remained behind her lids. She had not permitted the images their due since her early days at Darcy House, and so she studied them through the blurry lens the pounding in her head provided. A shaky image of her reading a letter, anger marking her features, quickly faded into one of her husband, his features now so dear to her, the look of longing upon his face. As if wiped away with a dusty rag, she next saw herself running—not exactly viewing her stride, but rather, hearing her labored breathing and noting the blurred images as she pushed through a crowd. People quickly stepping from her way. And William's voice calling her name. And then feeling herself falling, which was followed by blackness.

Her chest heaved, as if she had actually been running. The pain of moments ago had subsided, and she slowly opened her eyes to view the now familiar bed drape in her quarters at Pemberley. Her hand reached out, as if by its own accord, to feel the mattress on the right, half expecting to encounter the warmth of William's sturdy chest, but then she recalled he had gone to Manchester. "Hurry your return, my love," she whispered to the empty space.

Before she could forget the dream, she closed her eyes again to capture the memories. "Obviously, my running had to do with the accident," she murmured so as not to disturb the cocoon that wrapped her in the bed's warmth. "But what of the one of William? Was that before we married or recently? And why did I appear so angry when reading the letter? Was the anger a result of what the letter held or a dislike for its author?" Elizabeth found her features drawing up in confusion. "Is this a true memory or one I have concocted in William's absence? Have I borrowed a memory in my search for myself?"

The door leading to the servant's entrance opened, and Hannah slipped quietly into the room. "Ah, you are awake?" The maid smiled kindly upon Elizabeth. "You asked me to wake you so you might have time to change your frock before supper."

Elizabeth frowned. "It seems foolish to put the staff to so much bother for just me. Would Cook be offended if I take a tray in my room? I cannot seem to muster the desire to dine alone."

"I am certain Cook will understand. Mrs. Reynolds earlier cautioned that you would likely be hesitant to sit to table with Mr. Darcy away from the estate."

Elizabeth rose from the bed. "I shall be thankful for Miss Darcy's company tomorrow."

"The staff is pleased to have the Darcys at home for Christmastide." Hannah reached into the wardrobe and withdrew a soft green day dress.

"Mr. Darcy explained the reason for their absence since his father's death." Elizabeth permitted Hannah to undo the laces and assist her into the fresh gown.

"I shall inform Cook of your requiring a tray," Hannah said as she adjusted the green gown over Elizabeth's figure. "Perhaps you would enjoy a hot bath tonight before you retire."

Elizabeth's disposition brightened. "I would definitely like a bath. Thank you for thinking of me. I shall find a book in the library to read afterwards."

Hannah picked up the wrinkled gown to take with her to press later. "I shall return in a bit with the tray."

"I believe I will walk the gallery." Elizabeth laughed lightly. "I must learn more of the noble heritage into which I married."

"I doubt Mr. Darcy has a care to whether you can name his ancestors or not," Hannah observed. "The man be quite besotted by you."

Elizabeth paused to smile. "When I woke at Darcy House, I was quite frightened by his stern countenance. Now, his features are those I seek in the morning, when I wake, and at night before I turn to sleep."

"Has your memory returned?" Hannah questioned in hopeful tones.

Elizabeth paused, wondering whether to share news of her recent dream. "I recall running and Mr. Darcy calling my name."

Hannah nodded her encouragement.

"And there was one of Mr. Darcy looking upon me with fondness."

"Naturally," Hannah said with a soft giggle and a lift of her eyebrows.

Elizabeth hesitated before continuing. "There was another memory: This one of me. I am reading a letter, and I am very angry. Do you have suggestions as to why I was upset of anything of the letter's sender?"

Hannah paused as if deciding how to respond. Finally, she said, "Mr. Sheffield spoke once of a letter Mr. Darcy wrote to you. Evidently, there were several drafts, portions of them left unburned in the master's grate. As may be expected, Mr. Sheffield did not read the bits left behind, but your name was on one of the remnants. Perhaps what Mr. Darcy included in his letter upset you."

"Was this after you came into my service?"

"No. It was before you traveled to Derbyshire in August. I believe it was when you were at Rosings Park in Kent."

Elizabeth thought, *Likely something to do with Mr. Darcy's first proposal.* Therefore, she shook off the idea. "I do not think the letter Mr. Sheffield referenced was the one in my dream, for in the dream, I was wearing the purple gown, supposedly part of my trousseau. Naturally, in my dream I could have only thought my gown was purple, for we spoke of letting out the seam on it only yesterday, but I thought perhaps I wore the dress and read the letter some time during my wedding journey to Bath."

"I cannot say for certain, Mrs. Darcy, but permit me to ruminate on it. If I think of anything, I will come to you right away."

However, Elizabeth was not pleased with her maid's answer. She was certain that Hannah withheld information, and she wondered whether the letter had something more to do with Darcy than it did with her. Perhaps she had found an old love letter from a lady among his things. *From Mrs. Avendell?* The idea did not please her, at all. She glanced to the direction Hannah had gone. She must never forget that Hannah was Miss Darcy's servant long before she came to serve her. Since her childhood, in fact. Naturally, her maid's loyalty was first, and foremost, to the Darcys.

Chapter 10

WHEN DARCY ARRIVED IN Manchester, he made a show of calling upon his Uncle Matlock's banker and man of business, pretending he had questions regarding a recent investment he and Lord Matlock had made. In that manner, Darcy would not be forced to lie to Elizabeth again. He did not wish to base his marriage on untruths.

On the morning following his journey to Manchester, Darcy met with Cowan in a less than savory section of the city. "How long has Wickham been here?" Darcy asked. The odor of filth and human waste filled his nostrils.

"Three days." Cowan checked his ever-present journal. "Wickham left London a little less than a week past. First, he traveled to outside of Oxford, where he spent the night gaming and his day in bed with a woman known for her 'accessibility.'"

Darcy frowned. He did not wish to consider the diseases Mr. Wickham carried to Lydia Wickham's bed. He doubted his former friend ever considered a French sleeve or other means to avoid infection or conception. George Wickham constantly sought the thrill of a winning hand or a female conquest and the saints be demmed.

"And then he traveled straight to Manchester?"

"Mail coach. Only spent a night at an inn when he switched mail routes," Cowan reported with confidence.

"No one traveled with him? Do we know whether Mrs.

Wickham remains in Newcastle?" Darcy studied the building where Wickham had let a room and considered how far his childhood friend had sunk. He was certain George Darcy and the late Martin Wickham were looking down upon godson and son, respectively, in total dismay.

"Mrs. Wickham remains in Newcastle," Cowan reported. "Supposedly Lieutenant Wickham received permission from his commanding officer to return to Derbyshire for the pending death of his uncle."

"Wickham has no relations remaining unless reports of his mother's death some ten years prior were false. Even if such was true, a *mother* is not an *uncle*, and neither Martin Wickham nor the late Christine Wickham had brothers."

"Unfortunately, Lieutenant Wickham's captain learned the truth too late. His two weeks' approved absence has stretched into a month already."

"And appears to have no end," Darcy observed. With a heavy sigh, he suggested, "Perhaps I should make arrangements with Captain Deston to send Mrs. Wickham home to Mr. Bennet if Wickham does not return to Newcastle by the end of Christmastide. I would have Mrs. Wickham sent home sooner, but I suspect Mr. Wickham desires her abandonment."

Cowan remarked, "Might be a wise choice to keep her leave-taking an option, but not for Mr. Wickham's sake, but rather for the girl's."

"I will write to Father Bennet this evening to apprise him of Mr. Wickham's activities, as well as to make discreet inquiries into whether Mr. Wickham left his wife with enough funds to pay for her rooms and food."

Cowan cleared his throat to catch Darcy's attention. "I have a correction to my previous report, the one I presented you in London."

Darcy's eyebrow rose with interest. "And that would be?"

Cowan placed his journal in an inside pocket of his coat and looked Darcy in the eye, a move uncharacteristic of the majority of those he employed. In fact, few in society spoke to him without some degree of reverence. *Likely why Elizabeth Bennet interested me so completely. The woman did not fear me or show me deference.* "When Mr. Wickham was in London, he called often upon a woman," Cowan confessed. "At first, we assumed the woman was either Mrs. Younge or Mrs. Wickham, both women possess dark tresses, and so we erred when we heard Lieutenant Wickham kept company with a woman of that description."

"What else do we know of the woman?"

Cowan continued to keep Darcy's gaze. "Not much. She departed London the day before you set out for Dover."

"To where?"

"Matlock."

Darcy's frown deepened. "She was someone from Derbyshire? Someone with a prior relationship with Mr. Wickham?"

"Likely, sir. We managed to learn the woman's movements by following the routes of the coaching inns, but there was nothing after Matlock. She could live in the village, or she could have arranged private transportation from there. We know she did not hire a carriage or let a horse in Matlock."

Darcy's expression turned grim. "I do not like the idea of Mr. Wickham keeping company with any woman other than his wife. Do we know the woman's name?"

"At the hotel and with others on the coaching route, she used the name 'Mrs. Rosewood,' but my men have not found anyone of that name in and around Matlock that fits the woman's description."

"Which is?" Darcy inquired.

"Early to mid thirties, dark hair, and blue eyes."

"Likely hundreds who match that description," Darcy summarized.

Cowan stiffened, evidently holding himself to a high standard. "One more thing, sir."

Darcy inclined his head. "And that would be?"

"The woman was seen with Mr. Wickham on the street outside of Darcy House right before Mrs. Darcy's accident. We think she must have been the one who called at Darcy House before your arrival."

~~~

Elizabeth held her breath. The dream from the previous night had returned. Only this time, after reading the letter, she had violently wadded it up and marched across the room and tossed it in the fireplace, to watch it burn. She wished she could have leaned over her own shoulder to read what the letter held. *Could William know the contents?* she wondered, while not permitting even the slightest muscle to twitch, fearing if she did, the image she held behind her lids would skitter away before she could consider what it all meant.

The image of the paper going up in flames faded into the one where her husband looked upon her with such appreciation that Elizabeth felt warmth pool in her most private place. The flame marking the burning letter could now be viewed in the heat lingering in William's eyes. In some ways, she wished she could view herself as he did, but she suspected what had likely been her boldness would shock her.

In the next instant, she was running again, and Darcy was calling her name. She glanced over her shoulder in the direction of his voice, and the sun glared into her eyes, momentarily blinding her. An impact. Pain. Feeling herself falling. Blackness.

Disappointed in not discovering more of what had occurred, on a rush, she heavily expelled the breath she had held. "Obviously, William's version of what lies between us holds truth," she whispered. Not that she any longer held doubts of his affection for her, or, for that matter, her growing affection for him.

"Concentrate on one part of the memory," she told herself. "The letter." She suspected whatever was keeping her at a loss was tied to the letter's contents. "I will speak of it to William when he returns. Hopefully, I shared something of it with him."

~~~

Darcy stepped out onto the street. He had hoped for a bit of sun, but between the low clouds and the smoke seeping through

In Want of a Wife

the streets from the numerous factories, anything resembling warmth would be hard to purchase. He glanced about the street only to have his eyes land on George Wickham leaning against a post. "I believe my breakfast has taken a sour turn," Darcy grumbled.

"And I am pleased to see you as well, Darcy." Wickham stood and straightened the line of his uniform. "Might we talk?"

"If you insist," Darcy quipped, turning immediately to reenter the hotel. He did not look behind to observe whether Wickham followed or not. He could hear the lieutenant's tread on the stairs. Opening the door to his suite, he stopped in the room's middle and pivoted to face his long-time foe.

Wickham paused inside the door and looked about the room. Reaching behind him to close the door, he said, "Much better than my accommodations, but I expect you know that as you spent some time outside my let rooms yesterday with the man I assume is the one following me."

"And your point is?" Darcy snarled.

"Why are you having me followed, Darcy?" Wickham lifted an eyebrow in accusation.

"I was interested in why you left my wife's sister in an unfamiliar city with no family or friends to protect her," Darcy answered simply.

As was customary with his former friend, Wickham attempted to turn the conversation from his faults to those with whom he conversed. "I had forgotten Miss Elizabeth recently became Mrs. Darcy. As neither my wife nor I were asked to attend the nuptials, it is no wonder I had forgotten." Wickham's eyes scanned the room, as if assessing the value of each item. "Naturally, I was thankful not to be asked to perform my duty once again to the Darcy legacy, but, I will admit, I wish Father Bennet had granted Mrs. Wickham permission to return to Longbourn. My wife knew disappointment at being excluded, and when she is not happy, no one within hearing distance knows peace."

"Is such the reason you told your commanding officer of

the death of your 'uncle'?" Darcy accused.

Wickham shrugged off the charge against him. "You have spent your money well."

"I would prefer to spend my time and my wealth upon a more worthy cause," Darcy countered.

Something in his demeanor must have penetrated Wickham's defenses, for the lieutenant stilled. "My business is mine alone, Darcy. I did not ask for your so-called 'assistance' with my marriage to Lydia Bennet, nor did I ask for your interference in my dealings with my commanding officer. Moreover, I doubt Mrs. Wickham sought Mrs. Darcy's aid, for my wife trusts me."

Raw bitterness settled between them. "I imagine Mrs. Wickham does trust you. She is young and impressionable. However, I wonder how long your wife will accept your well-constructed lies when she learns you were not tending to a dying uncle, but, rather, were in London with another woman, not to mention your one night gambling away what was likely your rent,, and your day in the bed of a renowned doxy."

"And why do you care, Darcy? You have wished for some time to wash your hands of me. Why does the state of my marriage matter to you?" Wickham demanded. Familiar mocking tones laced Wickham's questions.

Irritation flashed through Darcy, but he swallowed his ready retort. He assumed an air of indifference. "You should care also," he took the offensive. "Your lieutenancy, your future occupation, and the money I settled upon Miss Lydia are all contingent upon the girl knowing satisfaction in her marriage."

"And why would you think any woman with whom I have shared intimacies would know anything less than *satisfaction*," Wickham countered.

Darcy swallowed the words rushing to his lips. He would not venture a guess as to why Elizabeth called out Wickham's name in her delirium: Despite his nature, he would not allow pessimism to prevail. He would accept her avowals of love and place his trust in Elizabeth's claim to know nothing of George Wickham. "Your amours may have known satisfaction with the act, but not with your lack of devotion afterwards. You forget, I have firsthand knowledge of how you regard your commitments to others. I have paid more than one father to cover your deception."

"Do you wish my expression of gratitude? We both know you acted to cover the smudge on your name, not mine."

"I want you to return to your wife and abide by the agreement you made with me and Mr. Gardiner." Later, he would renew his prayer never to encounter George Wickham again.

"It is my intention to begin my return to Mrs. Wickham later today."

"And your excuse for your captain?" Darcy demanded.

"I will assuage Captain Deston's concerns. Never you mind the excuse."

Darcy placed his gloves and hat on a nearby table. Regarding Wickham with a remarkable veil of self-possession, he said casually, "Then you will know no grievance on my part."

Wickham hesitated, a very telling point, before saying, "Welcome to the family, Darcy," a remark that his old friend thought would infuriate him, but Darcy had expected an exit salvo.

Demanding his expression remain unchanged, Darcy waited until Wickham turned to leave before he said, "I know of the woman who accompanied you about London. I know when you traveled here, and when she returned to Derbyshire. I know it all, Wickham."

Wickham did not turn around, but his response came with impressive speed. "If you knew everything, Darcy, you would be at Pemberley making your apologies to your new bride."

◈

"I plan to enjoy a walk," Elizabeth told Mr. Nathan. She had been most disappointed when Miss Darcy did not arrive yesterday as planned, and her restlessness had gotten the better of her. Surely Georgiana would make an appearance soon. Elizabeth did not like being alone at Pemberley. Doing so brought on a return of her fears of never recovering her memory.

The butler frowned. "It is not my place to prevent your doing so, but Mr. Darcy charged me and the rest of the staff with your safety, ma'am. Might I add a caution?" Reluctantly, she nodded her acceptance of his warning. "Pemberley is well-tended by the gardeners and groundskeepers, but there is much open land that holds dangerous trails and drop-offs unless one is familiar with the contour of the area."

Elizabeth wished to remind Mr. Nathan she was the estate's mistress and she could do as she pleased, but she knew the man was only following Mr. Darcy's instructions. "I do not mean to go far. Miss Darcy will hopefully arrive soon, and I wish to be here to greet her, but I require a stretch of my legs, or I might go mad." She added a smile to assure the man she spoke figuratively.

Mr. Nathan nodded his understanding. "Then perhaps you might choose to walk the entrance road. It is wide—properly graveled—nearly a mile to the gatehouse—possesses wonderful views of the parkland and the stream—"

"And I cannot become lost," Elizabeth finished.

"There is that also," Mr. Nathan said in practiced tones.

Elizabeth again smiled at the man. "Then fetch my pelisse and my muff, Mr. Nathan."

"Yes, ma'am."

Within five minutes, she was crossing the circular drive toward the bend in the road that hid the full grandeur of Pemberley from those who dared to arrive on the property without knowledge of Pemberley House, and even to those who called upon the estate on a regular basis.

As she walked briskly along, Elizabeth concentrated on each remarkable spot, often turning in place and pausing to admire the great variety of ground. Each step revealed more of the splendor into which she had married. "And of this place, I am to serve as mistress," she whispered in awe.

Finally, she reached a point where the woods began in earnest. It was a considerable eminence, and Elizabeth turned back to rest her eyes on Pemberley House, which was situated on the opposite side of the valley. Its greatness and its beauty had her swallowing a bit of trepidation rushing to her chest. The manor was a large, handsome stone building, imposing in the simplicity of its architectural lines, standing well on high ground, and backed by a ridge of woody hills, which she now recognized as part of the nature trail at the edge of the lawns. She thought there could be no other place for which nature had done more good.

With a sigh of satisfaction, she set her sights on the wooded area ahead. The walk was easy because she was walking downhill. She recalled when she arrived at Pemberley, Mr. Darcy's coach entered the park at a low point and slowly climbed to the manor house. "The return will require me to assume a slower pace," she said with a smile. The crisp air on her cheeks felt good, as did the freedom of the exercise. In spite of her infirmity, the Lord had blessed her. She paused to count God's favors. She closed her eyes and lifted her chin to speak to Heaven. "Thank you, God, for sparing my life and for bringing William into my world. I possess a loving and faithful husband who promises to protect both me and our family."

"Does he?"

Elizabeth's eyes sprang open. She turned frantically in circles, searching the thick woods for any signs of another person.

"Who is there? Show yourself," she demanded, but there was no movement — no other sound — not even the chirp of birds or the chatter of a squirrel — nothing but the soft snap of a twig and quick hitch of her breathing.

Suddenly frightened by the unknown, she hiked her skirt and made her feet move in the direction she had come. Constantly looking over her shoulder, she stumbled along the road she had enjoyed until this moment. "Be sensible," she silently chastised herself, but she did not slow down. The incline she had anticipated earlier caused her to labor, her chest heaving from the exertion.

Finally, she cleared the heavy woods, but she still did not feel safe. She silently cursed her response, but such did not slow her steps. She was in a strange place, a place she had visited previously, but of which she held no memory. Reaching the spot where she had previously viewed Pemberley in the distance, Elizabeth paused; bent over at the waist and hands braced on her knees, she struggled to capture her breath.

Then she heard it: a loud rumbling coming from the direction she had just fled.

Chapter 11

ELIZABETH CAUGHT AT HER chest to stifle the scream rushing to her lips. She knew she should run, but her feet would not respond. She simply stared in horror at the dark shadows of the woods, wondering what to do to protect herself, as the sound grew louder, whatever it was that stalked her, it was barreling straight at her.

As the sound surrounded her, swallowing her in its horror, Elizabeth squeezed her eyes shut and waited for the wall of fear to have its way with her.

Seconds crawled by as the air around her filled with loud shouts and shrill sounds of screams and the grinding of gravel. She wrapped her hands across her face and braced for impact.

"Ho!" a man screamed, but she made no move to save herself.

Suddenly, everything went quiet—not quiet exactly, for there was the whinny of horses and calls between several individuals asking if any were injured, but she still cowered where she was, refusing to look up, expecting the worst.

A jingle of what sounded of a harness was quickly followed by the sound of running feet, but before she could react, someone caught her up in an embrace.

"Elizabeth. Dear God, Elizabeth," a sweet feminine voice called as she rocked Elizabeth in place. "Tell me you are well."

Elizabeth opened her eyes to view a carriage and four. The

horses stomped in place in protest. Slack lines were untangled. A driver and footman in Darcy livery assisted a matronly woman from the coach. Her eyes slid to the girl bracing her against her chest. "Georgiana?"

"Yes." The girl heaved a heavy sigh. "What are you doing out here?"

Elizabeth shook her head to clear it and looked about in confusion. "I...I was taking a walk." She glanced to where Miss Darcy's companion walked stiffly toward them. "Mrs. Annesley," she called, "please say you are not injured." She glanced to the girl beside her. "And you, Georgiana? Are you well? Truly well? Mr. Darcy would never forgive me if I caused you injury."

The girl ignored Elizabeth's statement. Instead, she answered in calming tones, "We likely have a few bruises, but nothing traumatic." She slid her arm through Elizabeth's. "Why did you not move from the way when you heard my coach approach?"

Elizabeth's frown deepened. "I am not certain." Distractedly, she explained, "Mr. Nathan suggested I walk the main entrance road rather than the trails in Darcy's absence."

"William is not at Pemberley?" Georgiana inquired.

"In Manchester. On business." She looked around apologetically at all the chaos she had caused. "I am grieved by my actions."

"It is natural," Georgiana declared, clasping Elizabeth's hands in hers. "Especially after what happened to you in London. The sound of an approaching carriage must be terrifying under those circumstances. Under any circumstances," she was quick to say.

"Miss Darcy," the driver interrupted their conversation. "One of the horses will require additional care. I can fetch another horse from the barns, but it will take a bit of time to resume the journey."

Miss Darcy glanced to her companion. "If Mrs. Annesley is well enough to walk—" The lady in question nodded her agreement. "Then Mrs. Darcy, Mrs. Annesley and I will walk the rest of the way to Pemberley. I will have Mr. Nathan send grooms to assist you with the horses and the carriage, and others to assist Mr. Matthews with the luggage."

"Yes, Miss."

The man turned to leave, but Elizabeth caught his arm. "Please accept my sincerest apologies for the trouble I have caused you. Thank you for saving me from further injury, Mr. —"

"John Coachman, ma'am," the man provided.

Elizabeth shook off his response. "Such may suffice in other households, but I have yet to hear Mr. Darcy speak of any of his servants without using their surnames. Such is one of the qualities I admire about the man, and I mean to emulate him. Your name, sir?"

"Mr. Benson, ma'am."

Elizabeth nodded her thanks. "I shall have no difficulty recalling your name, Mr. *Benson*," she said in reassuring tones, while wishing for the ability to remember the rest of her history with such ease. I prefer to associate names to make them easier to recall. Before I was Mrs. Darcy, I was Miss *Ben*net." She smiled upon the man. "Thank you again for the care you and Mr. Matthews," she nodded to Georgiana's footman, "provide Miss Darcy and Mrs. Annesley."

"It is our privilege, ma'am."

Without discussing how they would proceed, Elizabeth and Georgiana each caught one of Mrs. Annesley's arms to support the woman's step, which still appeared a bit shaky, on the graveled path.

"When did William depart?" Miss Darcy asked as they crossed the bridge to turn toward Pemberley House.

"Three days prior. Your brother promised not to be gone for more than four, perhaps five, days," Elizabeth explained.

"And so you chose to walk *the main road?*" Georgiana asked with a lift of inflection in her voice, which caught Elizabeth's already present guilt and hitched it higher. Despite her earlier calm, her new sister-in-marriage was, obviously, experiencing difficulty in understanding what occurred moments earlier.

"As I have previously only once walked the lower trails with Mr. Darcy, Mr. Nathan suggested I might keep to the main road so as not to have a misstep." She chuckled ironically. "Little did he know I attract chaos."

Miss Darcy leaned forward to glance around Mrs. Annesley to say, "My coach's approach was not a misstep. After all you experienced in London—"

"But it was not your coach that first frightened me," Elizabeth declared.

Miss Darcy pulled her companion to a halt. "Then what brought on your fear?"

Elizabeth glanced around, feeling suddenly foolish. "It was nothing. I was being a ninny."

Mrs. Annesley shook her head in the negative. "I have had your acquaintance but a short time, Mrs. Darcy, but you do not strike me as foolish. Mr. Darcy, who is quite the intellect, would never present his hand to a woman who responded to the world in a witless manner. Such a woman would bore him to Bedlam."

"Your opinion of me would quickly change if you had viewed my earlier actions," Elizabeth argued.

"Then perhaps you should describe what occurred," Miss Darcy instructed.

"You will think it odd," Elizabeth prefaced, but when her companions remained silent, she explained. "I stopped along the wooded part of the lane. Silly as it may sound, I tarried to have a moment with God."

"You have suffered greatly in this recent matter," Miss Darcy said in sympathetic tones. "Taking a moment to offer your gratitude to God for His infinite mercy in all things does not appear odd, at all. Our Lord saw that no permanent harm had come to you."

Elizabeth blushed. "I did not thank God for my life, for I have done so many times since I awoke at Darcy House. Rather, I thanked God for your brother's role in my life. Without William's devotion, I would be lost."

"I am pleased you and he are finding new ground," Miss Darcy said. The satisfaction on the girl's countenance was unmistakable. Darcy's sister wished him to be happy, while Elizabeth simply prayed she could make him so.

Swallowing hard to drive away the flush of embarrassment rushing to her cheeks, Elizabeth continued. "I stopped and closed my eyes and lifted my face to the heavens. Then I spoke my pledge of gratitude."

"And then?" Miss Darcy whispered.

Elizabeth frowned in remembrance. "I thanked God for Mr. Darcy's affection, and someone in the forest asked if William truly loves me."

"Who?" Miss Darcy asked in urgency. The girl looked around as if someone could be lurking nearby, which heightened Elizabeth's anxiousness. "Did you recognize the person?"

"The person ignored my demands to appear before me, leaving me to shiver in fear. What alarmed me the most was the total silence. Nothing moved in the surrounding woods. Not a bird nor a rabbit. Just the soft click of a twig, indicating someone or something was truly there. I did not know what else to do; I ran away. I had just reached the clearance of the eminence when I heard your carriage. I am ashamed to say I permitted my imagination to expect a reoccurrence of what beset me in London. I was to be plowed down again."

Darcy quietly opened the door to his wife's bedchamber. With Wickham's departure, there was no reason for him to remain in Manchester, and so he pressed Mr. Farrin to reach Pemberley. Thankfully, the sky had cleared, and with a bright moon, they had arrived well after midnight, but safely so. Before Darcy could reach his room, Mr. Nathan informed him of the trouble Elizabeth had encountered upon Pemberley's main entrance.

Although he had told himself he would simply look in upon his wife and surprise Elizabeth in the morning, the account of her nearly being run over again demanded that he hold her in his arms. He could have lost her while he was away dealing with Wickham's latest manipulations. "No more," he whispered his promise to her and to himself. His duty was to his wife and his sister and, perhaps someday, his children. Mr. Bennet could address Lydia Wickham's disaster of a marriage.

Dropping his banyan across a chair, Darcy crossed to the bed and lifted the linens so he might settle beside his wife. Gathering Elizabeth closer, he kissed the back of her neck and snuggled into the scent of lavender on her skin.

"William?" she asked sleepily.

"Were you expecting someone else?" he whispered in her ear as he nuzzled closer still.

She turned in his arms. "Is it you?" She ran her fingers across his cheek. "You are real, are you not?"

"I am, love."

She gently kissed his lips, and Darcy sighed with satisfaction. She had not initiated any signs of affection for him since that last night they had been together in Bath. "You were missed, sir."

He kissed her forehead. "I told Mr. Farrin I could not spend another night away from my lovely wife."

She playfully slapped his shoulder. "Tell me you would not embarrass me as such," she charged.

He settled her upon her back and draped himself over her. "I did not say anything to belittle my wife," he assured her with a series of light kisses across her nose and over her cheekbones. "But I am certain my distraction and my counting off the miles told him all the man needed to know." Darcy kissed her gently. "Now, why do you not tell me what happened today?" It was not his intention to question her when he crawled into Elizabeth's bed, but he would not sleep until he knew how she had fared with today's incident. "I will remain silent, and you may tell me what occurred in your own manner."

"No questions?" she asked on a soft sob.

"No interruptions," he corrected. "I will save my questions for later."

Elizabeth presented him a curt nod before burying her

face into his shoulder. Her tale touched his heart twice: First, when she described thanking God for his place in her life, and then again when she described her flight from the woods and the terror of Georgiana's coach set to run her over.

"Your sister says Mr. Benson is one of the best," she finished.

Darcy would see that Benson had something extra in the Christmas pouch Darcy would present the man. "He is exceptional. I would not trust Georgiana's safety with anyone less."

They were silent for a moment, each lost in his thoughts. At length, Darcy asked, "Was the person's voice one you recognized?" In spite of fighting the thought, he could not help but wonder if Wickham had made a stop at Pemberley on his return to Newcastle. Wickham's horse would have made better time than would have Darcy's coach. Naturally, one of Cowan's men trailed Wickham, but Darcy's former friend knew all the trails around Pemberley, as well as Darcy. Wickham could easily lose even the best of Cowan's men.

Elizabeth said cautiously, as if remembering what occurred. "There was nothing familiar about the person's voice."

Darcy said a silent prayer: Please do not permit her to say Mr. Wickham's name again. "Could you tell something of his accent? Tenor or baritone or bass? Cultured or a villager or even a tenant?"

She looked up at him in what the shaft of moonlight streaming through the drapes declared to be amusement. "Who said the voice belonged to a man?"

Chapter 12

"I WANT THIS WHOLE area searched," Darcy ordered. "Look for footprints. The ground should still be damp from the recent rains."

"We looking for a poacher?" Mr. Porter, his gamekeeper asked.

"I am not certain," Darcy admitted.

Earlier, he and Elizabeth had walked the same path she had taken yesterday. His wife had been quite surprised when he chose to believe she had actually heard a person in Pemberley Woods. "Naturally, I believe you," he had assured her. "Why would I not?"

She cautiously reminded him. "You did not believe my memory loss."

"You are correct," he declared. "It took me longer than it should have to accept the fact I did not properly care for my wife. My denials had more to do with my failures than your honesty."

"You did not fail me," Elizabeth argued.

"I did," he insisted. "But I shan't do it again."

And he would not permit her to face the world's troubles again. He would place himself between her and those who meant her harm.

"Mr. Darcy!" Porter called. "Over here."

Darcy left the graveled path to enter the thick growth of the trees to find Porter and one of his men kneeling beside a patch of grass, obviously, recently trampled down. "What have you found?"

Porter frowned. "Not an animal, sir. See how the grass be bent outward as if whatever stood here be turnin' in a circle. Don't know many animals that step close together in a circle, exceptin' a dog or a cat attemptin' to find a place to lie down."

"But a dog or a cat turns only once or twice," Darcy observed.

"And they not weigh enough to bend tall grass flat," his man added.

Porter employed a stick to lift several blades of grass. "Some sort of boot print. Not very large." Even before Porter made his next statement, Darcy knew Elizabeth had been correct. "Appears to be a youth or a woman. The heel is not wide enough for a man."

Darcy agreed. "I want you to follow the person's tracks. Bring out the hounds if you think it necessary. I would like to know who this person is. Follow the trail. Did the person go farther inland or back to the main road? Also, ask at the gatehouse. See if anyone noted a stranger — someone not with business at Pemberley — in the area yesterday."

"And what have we here?" he asked upon entering his wife's sitting room.

Elizabeth glanced up with hope, but he shook off her unstated question. She nodded her understanding. "Mrs. Annesley and the maids are making birthing gowns for the five families who will deliver a child this winter. Georgiana thought it would be appropriate if she and I added a bit of embroidery to the hem and sleeve." She held up the gown upon which she had applied her needle for his inspection.

"It was Mrs. Annesley's idea," Georgiana explained in excited tones. "My companion thought, in the future, we could create a supply of gowns to be given to the parents with the welcome baskets Pemberley customarily presents the families."

Darcy smiled at his sister. She might have secretly thought

to offer a fairing to his cottagers before Elizabeth joined the family, but she would never have acted upon her ideas, for she was too shy, a family trait. "I am quite proud of you, Georgie."

"Are you not proud of me, also, Mr. Darcy?" his wife asked with a simple taunt. He enjoyed the idea that her injury had not affected her personality.

"I adore you, Mrs. Darcy," he said with a knowing gaze.

"And you no longer adore me," Georgiana said with a giggle.

Darcy laughed. "I see how it is to be. You two will distract me until I no longer know north from south. I am equally proud of both of the Darcy ladies, and my adoration will never fail either of you."

Georgiana shot a quick glance to Elizabeth. "We can finish the last two gowns tomorrow. You and Darcy should enjoy the gardens. At the gatehouse yesterday, Mr. Spurlock told me we will have snow by Wednesday."

"Spurlock's rheumatism again?" Darcy teased.

Georgiana set her sewing basket aside. "Mr. Spurlock's aching joints are never in error. Now if you will pardon me."

"Enjoy your practice time," Darcy said with a grin.

Georgiana smiled also. "I always do." Her gaze slid from his to settle on Elizabeth. "Enjoy your walk, Brother."

With his sister's exit, Darcy caught Elizabeth to him. "I missed you, wife."

She chuckled. "It has only been a matter of hours since you left my bed."

"I never tire of your nearness." He feathered a kiss across her brow before resting his chin on the top of her head.

She sighed heavily. "Come." She stepped from his loose embrace to catch his hand. "Tell me what you have learned."

He hesitated. "Do you not wish to walk the garden?"

Her frown said it all. "If you are stalling, then you do not possess good news."

Darcy shrugged his response. "It is not what you wished."

Elizabeth sat heavily upon the settee. "I am not certain what I wished. I certainly did not want to hear of something sinister going on at Pemberley."

"Then you will be pleased to know it was all a misunderstanding." He caught her hand in his two. "As I promised this morning, I set men to search the area you indicated as being the spot you heard the voice. Within a few minutes, Mr. Porter, my gamekeeper, lit upon a patch of well worn grass and a partial boot print. Porter sent for a couple of dogs, and we began to follow the trail, which eventually led to the home of one of my cottagers."

"One of your tenants?" she asked. "A female?"

"Not exactly," he confessed.

"I do not understand."

"When we called upon the Camerons, it was young Edgar Cameron, who proved to be the scent the dogs had followed. Edgar admitted to being in the area yesterday. It seems the boy was chasing his new dog the family is training to herd the sheep. Edgar has named the dog *Dusty*."

"Does he?" she repeated. "You think I misunderstood what I heard? If so, why did the boy not show himself when I demanded he do so?"

"That I cannot answer. Edgar swears he did not see anyone on the road — claims he was only near the entrance road for less than a minute. He called out for the dog, spotted it nearby, and rushed off to catch the animal."

"It all appeared so real," she whispered in uncertainty. Earlier, after William had encouraged her to show him where she had encountered an unknown person in the woods, she had thought to share the recurring dream with him, but as her waking encounters proved false, how would he receive the news of a dream that did not make sense even to her? Their time together had fallen into a comfortable existence; she did not wish to return to their continuous arguments. She placed a small smile upon her lips. "It grieves me to have put you to so much trouble."

"Nothing concerning my wife is trouble," he assured her. "Even if the result is not what you suspected, I am pleased we have a resolution. I would not have you fear your days at Pemberley."

It was decided the Darcys would host a small supper party after the New Year, but before Twelfth Night. Darcy had insisted upon their limiting the number of guests. "I will not tolerate Elizabeth wearing her reserves thin," he had declared when Georgiana presented him a list of potential guests. Scanning the list, he drew lines through several names. "We should keep the number to fewer than twenty. Personally, I would prefer no more than a dozen."

"Why so few?" Georgiana ventured.

Elizabeth smiled upon the girl, who had quickly become her new confidante.

"First," her husband instructed, "we are well into the second week of December. Expecting people to change their festive days' plans to accommodate the Darcys is poor manners. Secondly, we must consider the date of the full moon to aid in travel. That being said, as we do not plan to house overnight visitors due to unexpected weather or travel troubles, we should keep the list restricted to our closest neighbors and perhaps those of prominence in Lambton."

"Do you not despise it when your brother is so practical," Elizabeth teased to soften any disappointment Miss Darcy might have experienced with Darcy curtailing some of the girl's plans.

"He would make our father proud," Georgiana declared. From her husband's expression, like her, Darcy did not know whether his sister's words were criticism or not.

Fortunately, Darcy chose to take up a congenial tone. "And likely drive Lady Anne to distraction. You are more of our mother's nature, Georgiana."

Miss Darcy smiled wistfully, "I wish I possessed a memory of my own of her." Realizing what she had said, the girl reached for Elizabeth's hand. "I apologize. I did not think whether my words would cause you pain before I said them."

Elizabeth squeezed the back of the girl's hand. "Although I pray each day for a different outcome, I cannot control my future unless I abandon my past. I will have the perfect wish for the new year. Instead of regretting my past mistakes, I shall simply declare the prospects of the next year as being the best for which I can hope."

Mr. Spurlock's prediction for a change in the weather arrived the following day. The snow, beginning in earnest some time overnight, greeted them with nearly two inches upon the ground by the time Elizabeth pulled back the drape to take in the morning sun.

"It is snowing, William," she said with a smile of delight.

Darcy stretched his arms over his head before using the pillows to prop himself up in bed. "Nothing from the ordinary in Derbyshire in December. We are accustomed to it."

"But I am not," she reminded him.

"Surely you recall something of snow." He looked upon her oddly.

"Obviously, I must know of snow," she corrected. "Otherwise, I would not recognize the white coating upon the ground, but while you consider snow in Derbyshire ordinary, for me, it is *extraordinary*. I would imagine Hertfordshire is more temperate than Derbyshire. How often could I have experienced snow? Perhaps once a year, at best."

"You do not recall walking in the snow? The cold biting your cheeks?"

"Not in the least," she responded after considering his question carefully.

Her husband barked a laugh. "Do you mean I will have the pleasure of introducing my beautiful wife to her first snowfall?"

"Only if you drag yourself from the bed and be about your duties to the estate now, so we might enjoy the snow later," she announced as she ripped the sheet from his body and caught his hand to tug him from the bed.

Darcy laughed at her efforts before jerking her down beside him, bracing himself above her. "You promise you will not go out into the snow until I can accompany you."

A frown formed upon her lips. "I shall not again be imagining someone set upon doing me harm."

It was her husband's turn to frown. "Such was not part of my request. I simply wish to share your first moments in the snow with you. Unfortunately, I cannot think to be away from my meeting with Mr. Scott, who has for years protested the boundary between his property and mine, until, at least, eleven, perhaps twelve of the clock. He is not a man with whom it is easy to reason. Say you will wait for me, Elizabeth."

"Naturally, I will wait to share the moment with you," she said in all seriousness.

He grinned conspiratorially. "No dumping snow upon my head when I am not looking."

The idea delighted Elizabeth, but she was not certain how William would react to mischief. "Only if you swear the same, sir."

As he had predicted. Mr. Scott proved difficult, but Darcy had remained adamant against the possibility of Scott using part of Pemberley's upper meadows for his sheep. The man had always been intractable, and Darcy would not reward him by quickly giving sway.

By the time he escorted his wife across the snow-covered lawn of Pemberley, the thick snow clouds had departed, leaving behind perhaps three inches. The snow was not the heavy, debilitating kind they would likely experience in January or February, especially along the upper peaks, but it was more than adequate for Elizabeth's first snowball battle, for, most assuredly, they would draw sides in a grand fight. Darcy had planned nothing less, and he was certain his wife had ruminated on the idea of dumping snow on his head since he had mentioned it earlier. Elizabeth Darcy was always in for a good match, whether it be checkers, chess, or snowballs.

"I love it, William," his wife said with a deep sigh of satisfaction. "Do you know whether I enjoyed snowstorms in Hertfordshire?"

He glanced down at the happiness marking her features. "I imagine you have known pleasure in a few of them. As you said earlier, you likely have not known snow as often as have I. Yet, I have no doubt you will easily become accustomed to it as part of your new life." He paused to catch a low-hanging branch. "If you held such memories," he said with a chuckle, "you would know better than to walk beneath a low bough covered in snow." She glanced up at him, confusion crossing her features a moment before he tapped the branch to send snow sprinkling down upon her upturned face.

"William!" she screeched as she used her gloves to dash away the onslaught of cold attacking her. "How could you?"

He laughed easily. "I could not resist, love. You were so innocently adorable."

She fussed at him. "I shall never be caught unawares again."

"Excellent," he declared boldly. "Then what say you to a bit of a contest?"

"What type of contest?" she asked skeptically.

He caught her hand and forced her to kneel beside him. "A battle in the snow. This was always one of my cousins' and my favorite winter activities." He would not tarnish this moment by the mention of George Wickham's part in those many snowball fights. "Lindale and Fitzwilliam were most masterful opponents. Naturally, you will not be equal in your skills, but that is to be understood."

As Darcy expected, his wife took umbrage with his words. "Why? Because I am a woman?"

"Certainly, for my cousins are stronger than you." He omitted the obvious fact he also was physically stronger than she.

"But I am more cunning," she declared boldly. It did

his heart well to hear something of the woman he married still buried within the woman who had lost everything. As sad as her injury made him, Darcy relished the idea of sharing with her many things she had forgotten.

He formed several snowballs and placed them on the ground before her, showing her how to squeeze the ball tightly so it would hold together. "We will *playfully* toss these balls at each other until one of us surrenders."

"I shall gladly accept your submission, although I know it will be painful for you to admit defeat to a mere woman," she taunted.

He chuckled easily. "Not so quick, my love."

She leaned forward as if to kiss him. Darcy instinctively closed his eyes to accept the gift of her affection. Instead, she jammed one of the snowballs he had made for her into his face.

Darcy sputtered and cleared the cold mess from his vision. "You vixen!" he called as he struggled to his feet, only to find Elizabeth had grabbed three of the snowballs he had formed, leaving behind the sausage-shaped ones she had made, before scrambling away from him.

"I apologize, William," she called, as her precious laughter filled his heart with happiness. "We women are often clumsy. I must have fallen into you."

"You fell into my face?" he taunted. "With a snowball?"

"Avoid the distractions." She turned gleefully in a small circle. "Your cousin, the colonel, would warn you as such."

"You should hide, Mrs. Darcy," he playfully called after her. "For you have declared war." Grabbing the three "sausage" balls she left behind, Darcy formed them into one compact snowball. Then he made a few reserves before he stamped off after her. He heard her laugh as she disappeared around the corner of the house.

Darcy followed her tracks across the lawn until he also reached the corner. Carefully edging around the house, he found there was no sign of her. "Where is she?" he grumbled right before the creak of the branches above his head announced his wife's location, but the realization arrived too late to prevent the rush of snow from covering his head and seeping beneath his coat.

"First strike!" she declared as she dropped to the ground — all skirts and a splash of color — before him. She darted away as he grabbed for her. "Do not trust a lady, Mr. Darcy," she called over her shoulder as she headed for the elaborate maze he had installed several years back to please his sister.

"You may have won the skirmish," he called after her, "but the victory will still be mine." He watched her go as he shook the snow out of his coat.

A burst of laughter from the entrance to the maze brought lightness to his soul. They both required this distraction from what was consuming too much of their time of late. After all, he was a newly married man, not a grandfather of a dozen children. "You have erred, my Lizzy," he said smugly as he approached the maze. "There is only one way in and one way out, and you must come past me to leave. I will be waiting for you."

"I am counting on it, William," she sing-songed from the other side of the hedgerow.

He reached through the holly in a fake attempt to grab her. As he thought, she squealed in delight, before arcing a snowball over the bush at him. Fortunately, he stepped back just in time to have it land at his feet. "A miss," he teased, "but an excellent attempt."

"I have two more and more than a dozen benches and statues from which to make additional weapons of out of the cold." Her voice came from deeper in the maze.

Darcy laughed before casually following the familiar path to the maze's center. In winter, the way was made clearer by the lack of vegetation and flowering vines. "Do not rush, love," he instructed as he continued his slow progress. "I do not want you too weak to put up a defense when I overtake you."

"I look forward to the contest, William," she responded.

And so he followed the prescribed paths until he reached the maze's center. Instead of his wife lying in wait to pelt him with snowballs, as he had expected, she sat upon a bench which she had wiped clean. "What is this?" he asked wondering what scheme she practiced.

"A surrender, William," she said sweetly and then waved a white handkerchief before her.

"Why do I not believe you, love?" he said suspiciously as he approached.

"Perhaps you know me better than I do myself," she countered. She reached out a hand to him.

Darcy knew he would probably regret accepting the gesture, but he did so, nevertheless, tugging her to her feet to stand before him. Desire warring with his good sense, he dropped the snowballs he had carried to gather her into his embrace. "I find it hard to believe Elizabeth Bennet Darcy would surrender so easily."

"Why is that?" she said softly. Her fingers crawled up his arm.

"Because my sweet Elizabeth's courage always rises with every attempt to intimidate her." He jammed his fingers into the thickness of her hair and caressed the nape of her neck. The heat between them affected his breathing. And hers. He kissed her temple and slid his lips over her cool cheek to perch about her mouth. One of her hands rested upon his chest. His free hand slid to the base of her spine to edge her closer to him. His heart pounded in his ears.

His possession of her mouth lacked the usual self control simply because Elizabeth appeared to welcome it. Their tongues tangled, and his wife caught the lapels of his jacket beneath his greatcoat. The heat of her closeness had warmed him despite the cold.

At length, he drew in a sharp breath. "It is I who surrenders, Elizabeth. You conquered my heart long ago. I was vanquished before I knew what had occurred." Slowly, he drew back, permitted inches to form between them. "Come, love. We should return to the house and change out of these wet clothes." He interlaced their fingers and turned to retrace his steps, but his wife, obviously, was not as distracted as he was.

She tugged on his hand as if her footing had slipped. As he turned to save her from another disaster, her left hand, the one she had held against the back of his coat, but never touching his body during their kiss shoved another snowball into his face. "Strike two!" she called as she rushed toward the exit. "And thus the victory!"

Darcy did not know whether to be angry or laugh. He chose the latter. "Thank you, Elizabeth," he called in jovial tones. "For the lesson in strategy, but, more importantly, for the cold delivered at your hands. You did me a service, love. I needed to cool down."

Chapter 13

BY THE NEXT DAY, the snow was gone, but her husband had promised there would be more snow and a rematch, and he would seek his revenge at that time. The idea pleased her because their battle in the snow was a memory no one would ever steal away from her.

Their days had become more routine. Darcy spent part of each day speaking about their past. Some of his tales shocked her: The idea of her impertinence took Elizabeth by surprise and then amazement, because her wonderful husband turned each tale into one where he swore to have enjoyed her "abuse." She was a most fortunate woman to claim Fitzwilliam Darcy's devotion.

She cried when he described her first refusal of his hand, mainly, for the time they had lost as a couple, but, also, and more importantly, for how he had suffered at her hands, but still managed to forgive her and love her more dearly.

When he had described the letter that had changed her opinion of him, Elizabeth briefly wondered if such was the letter she read that had made her so angry, but her wearing the purple gown in the vision eliminated Mr. Darcy's letter being the same one she had burned in her most recent dream. Moreover, he had told her, "I asked you to destroy the letter, for there were some expressions which might justify your despising me, and you indicated you would consider doing so, but I found it among your things after your accident."

A bit of Elizabeth took umbrage at his going through her belongings, for she had no doubt, he had searched for the connection between her and Mr. Wickham, but, after analyzing his reaction and the likely devastation he knew at her injury, she came to the conclusion she might have done the same if the tables had turned.

While Darcy was out on the estate one day, Elizabeth locked herself in her room and, with the strongest curiosity, read the letter several times, each reading increasing her wonder.

Thankfully, her husband had explained his initial objection to his friend Mr. Bingley marrying her sister Jane before Elizabeth had read the letter. However, without a memory of her supposed close relationship with her elder sister, Elizabeth viewed Darcy's objections as sensible, and all his protests were for naught. Her allegiance rested with him.

The fact he had trusted her with the tale of Mr. Wickham's ultimate betrayal dumbfounded her, especially in the light of her adamant refusal of his hand. His doing so spoke of the honor that ran through her husband's veins. Even after she had declared him to be the last man she would marry, he ceremoniously placed his sister's reputation in her hands, rather than to permit her to return to Hertfordshire without a fair warning of Mr. Wickham's proclivity for mischief and untruths. Darcy had loved her enough to place her future before his own comfort. "He continues to do the same each day I am here. In essentials, my husband is very much what he claims to be."

Reading Mr. Darcy's letter became a bridge between her past and her present, and, hopefully, a door to her future. When she considered how unjustly she had condemned and upbraided him, Elizabeth's anger turned inward, declaring herself unworthy of Darcy's love. His continued attachment excited gratitude, and his general character demanded her respect.

The Christmas season arrived at Pemberley with renewed happiness. As it had been five years since the Darcys had been at home for Christmas, Mrs. Reynolds insisted on plenty of greenery decorating the halls and the mantelpieces and staircases. Holly and red ribbons abounded.

"It is so beautiful," Elizabeth said as she snuggled into Darcy's embrace when the candles in the entranceway were lit for the first time, displaying the hall in all its glory. The Yule log was set ablaze at midnight to welcome in the festive days.

"Mrs. Reynolds outdid herself," Darcy said in satisfaction.

Therefore, Elizabeth awoke with a happy heart on Christmas morning. Hope for all her tomorrows had found a home at Pemberley. As was his custom, Darcy had risen before her to dress and go below, where he would greet her in the morning room.

Elizabeth stretched leisurely before reaching across the bed to discover whether her husband's heat still warmed the bed linens. Today, it did not, and she found herself frowning, wishing he was still close enough, so she might call him back so she could again take advantage of his loving embrace. With a sigh of disappointment, she rolled to her side, only to come across a piece of paper folded over several times and resting on Darcy's pillow.

She shoved herself to a seated position and draped the bed linens across her lap. Smoothing her hair into some sort of order, Elizabeth paused to settle her breathing and then unfolded the letter from her husband. The idea he would address her thusly filled her with something more than anticipation, leaving her without words to describe the elation filling her soul.

With a deep sigh of satisfaction, she read:

Good morning, my charming wife...

As this is the beginning of our first Christmas together, I wished to take a moment to recognize the wonder which fills my heart when I look upon your beautiful face. Even with our recent trials, I cannot think of spending another day on this earth without you by my side. My life before taking your acquaintance was filled with nothing but duty. You are the candle lighting my way in the darkness – leading me away from the loneliness. I want to be the man with whom you discover love.

I desire to some day know a smile you saved purely for me. I want to memorize every moment we share — to celebrate the amazing woman who is my wife.

Certainly, we will occasionally know heartbreak, but we also will know laughter and happiness and family. You are the air I breathe. Each moment without you is a punishment to me. I never thought to know love — to be worthy of someone's devotion — and I am grateful for your growing affection for me.

D

Elizabeth had no time to consider Darcy's words, for a soft knock announced Hannah's arrival.

"I am glad you be awake, ma'am." Hannah placed a gown across the back of a chair. It was the one they had decided upon for Elizabeth to wear to services today. Elizabeth quickly refolded Darcy's note.

"Am I required elsewhere?" she asked.

Hannah blushed, but she answered properly. "It is nearly half past eight, ma'am, and Mr. Darcy wishes to leave for services at ten."

Elizabeth hid her amusement. "I am assuming Mr. Darcy sent you to rouse me out." She crawled from the bed to stand beside it.

Hannah turned her back to disguise her chuckle. "I told Milly my mistress would be awake, while Miss Darcy prefers her sleep."

Elizabeth turned to place Darcy's letter in the drawer of her desk. She would secure it later. "Are you and Milly competing to have your mistress first to join Mr. Darcy at table? Am I to be subjected to speed rather than care on this Christmas day?" she asked in her customary teasing tones.

"There might be the matter of an extra dish of Christmas pudding," Hannah admitted.

Elizabeth laughed easily. "Then be about it. Do not let it be said I denied my maid her due simply by being difficult."

With tight precision, she and Hannah set about preparing

Elizabeth for the day's activities. They had planned for her to wear the same basic gown of forest green with three different overlays and a change of gloves and jewelry. Dressed, at last, Elizabeth sat at her dressing table, so Hannah might style her hair. "Not too elaborate," Elizabeth insisted. "I do not wish to spend the entire day regretting how tightly my curls are pinned to my head."

"I will leave a few loose curls to frame your face. The master seems to prefer your hair that way. Your appearance at your exchange of nuptials was the first time I ever viewed Mr. Darcy appear weak in his knees. The delicate lace veil your Aunt Gardiner had draped over your head had you taking on the aura of an angel come to earth. I am certain the master sees you as such in his dreams, although I would imagine in those dreams your lovely hair is down, rather than done up as elaborately as Mrs. Bennet ordered me to do on that day. Men appear to think a woman's hair a symbol of their glory. You certainly bewitched the master proper," Hannah said as she sent the brush the length of Elizabeth's hair.

"Thank you, Hannah, for sharing your recollections of that day. Of all my time with Mr. Darcy, such is one of the memories for which I most pray to have restored to me," Elizabeth said softly.

"It, and many more, will be," Hannah insisted.

"But it has been—" Elizabeth paused to calculate the number of weeks since she exchanged vows with Mr. Darcy.

Hannah paused also. "Fifty days."

Elizabeth frowned in disbelief. "Fifty days? My goodness. The time has raced by."

Hannah paused, as if wishing to speak openly. "Ma'am, would you mind answering a question?"

Elizabeth smiled kindly on the maid. "It would seem we are often asking questions of each other. What is it you wish to know?"

Hannah ventured cautiously, "Is there any hope you might know something of your monthlies, ma'am? I was just thinking that fifty days be a long time—" Her maid appeared as embarrassed by the question as Elizabeth was shocked by it. "At Mr. Darcy's request, I began taking care of you some two weeks before your marriage." In the mirror, Elizabeth watched as Hannah blushed. "To the best of my knowledge, there has been no proof of your not being enceinte. Could it be, ma'am?"

Elizabeth swallowed hard. *Could, she, even now, be carrying William's child?* Again, she counted back. According to her husband, they were last together intimately the day before her accident. *Forty-four days prior. Six weeks.* She required time to consider this turn of events. "Significant number of days to think me with child." The realization shook her to her core. *How could she take care of a child if she had no memories to share with it?* "I cannot tell Mr. Darcy of our suspicions until I am certain."

Hannah frowned. "The master has a right to know if you carry his heir," the maid argued.

"I will tell him, but not yet? Permit me to wait until after Twelfth Night ends." She rushed to make an explanation for her reluctance. "Mr. Darcy will cancel our first entertainment if he thinks the combination of my injury and a baby would again put me in danger. I do not wish to hide away from my responsibilities to Pemberley," Elizabeth pleaded. "Twelve days of Christmastide. If I am as we suspect, twelve days will make little difference."

"I do not like deceiving Mr. Darcy," Hannah said in stubborn tones.

"Neither do I," Elizabeth stated. "But I require time to accept all this as I should. If I am uncertain, then Mr. Darcy will become even more stubborn than he has been of late regarding my health."

Christmas Day began, as it should, at church. Sitting beside her husband in the Darcy pew, Elizabeth could not keep her mind on the cleric's Christmas message. Instinctively, her hand came to rest above her midsection. *A baby.* Was she prepared to know a child? Be a mother? A quick glance to her husband's profile said

Mr. Darcy would be a wonderful father. The idea pleased her. Of all the men she could have married, she had chosen one of God's best. She slipped her hand into his, and he turned to smile upon her, before resting their clasped hands upon his thigh.

Afterwards, he introduced her to the three families he had determined would be the best for her first venture as Pemberley's hostess. As her husband had expected, all three accepted on the spot. They left them with promises of sending around the written invitation after the tenants' celebration on the twenty-sixth.

"Mr. and Mrs. Logan and his sister appeared pleased for the invitation," Georgiana remarked once they returned to their coach.

"They have not long been in Derbyshire," Darcy explained. "I know Logan from our days at university. For many years, along with his uncle, he oversaw the family's interest in Somerset. He and the new Mrs. Logan returned to Derbyshire last February with the passing of his father. I suspect the gentleman and Mrs. Logan have had few opportunities to socialize with those not his father's former associates."

"Is Mr. Logan your age?" Elizabeth asked. Privately, she thought it would do both her and Darcy good to claim the couple as confidants if they proved to be congenial and trustworthy. For herself, she would like to have a married woman with whom she could discuss the trials of making a marriage work and something of childbirth.

"He was two years behind me at university, but we often came across each other in the library and spent time sharing news of Derbyshire."

Later, after a delicious midday meal, Darcy asked Mr. Nathan to gather the staff in the ballroom, where her husband ceremoniously recognized each of his servants with a small cloth pouch, which expressed his gratitude for the person's service to Pemberley. He shook the hand of each man and pressed Elizabeth to do the same for the female employees, while Georgiana presented each staff member with the pouch bearing coins. Elizabeth wondered when her husband had organized the additional salary for each person serving either inside or outside of Pemberley proper. Thinking upon it, she realized such was a means where she could ease her husband's responsibilities. She could assume the task for next year. It also occurred to her there must be other such duties. Whether she carried Darcy's child or not, she was his wife, and they must equally share in their future.

"We be most glad to have the master home, ma'am. It be too long—" or a similar statement was repeated by each of the women and several of the men as they received their Christmas tidings.

"You have earned the regard of a great man, ma'am," Mrs. Reynolds whispered as she accepted a brief hug from Elizabeth.

"I am well aware of Mr. Darcy's worth," Elizabeth responded, "but I appreciate knowing others view him as do I."

Once the servants were excused to enjoy their own celebrations below stairs, Georgiana asked, "May we open gifts now?"

Darcy laughed. "Are you not the greedy one?"

Georgiana protested, "I wish to view the expression on your and Elizabeth's faces when you open the items I chose for you, as much as I wish to see what you chose for me."

"A very noble endeavor," Mr. Darcy teased his sister as he directed her steps toward the family's favorite drawing room.

It was then they realized Elizabeth did not follow. Her husband appeared perplexed. "Is something amiss?" he asked gently.

Elizabeth blushed. "I have but the one gift I purchased in Lambton for Georgiana, and it is still upstairs in my desk. I did not think—"

"There are most assuredly fairings from you for both Georgiana and me in the drawing room," her husband insisted.

"I do not recall purchasing any such gifts," she argued.

"There were gifts in the things you had shipped to Pemberley before we married," he explained. "You also purchased items for your family, which you left in Mrs. Bingley's care, so do not think you might have forgotten those at Longbourn.

Unfortunately, the box bearing the items for Pemberley was accidentally dropped from the back of the wagon upon which it rested. The box cracked open. My servants reported the incident to me, and I oversaw the transfer of your things to a new crate." He stepped closer to speak privately to her. "Such is when I discovered you had kept my letter to you while at Rosings Park in a tight bundle with other notes and letters from your family."

Elizabeth felt the tears rush to her eyes. Her husband had not purposely betrayed her privacy. For always treating her honorably, she wished to throw her arms about his neck and kiss him thoroughly. Instead, she reached for his hand. "The gifts will be as much of a surprise to me as they will be to you."

Georgiana grinned at them. "I am assuming you did not purchase cologne for me or my brother or else Darcy or one of his men would have noted the aroma."

"Do not make assumptions, my dear, for they may come back to haunt you," Darcy said with an answering smile. "Did Mr. Chadwick say anything of broken bottles to you?"

Georgiana led the way to the drawing room. "No. But perhaps Mr. Chadwick kept quiet because he preferred the smell of your sandalwood or of my lemons to that of his mules."

She excused Hannah early. The day had been one of wonder, and Elizabeth required a few moments to digest all the revelations that had been delivered to her threshold today. She glanced to the door separating her quarters from that of her husband's. "Such a good man," she whispered. "Mr. Darcy deserves better than he received from me."

Again, her hand settled upon her stomach. As much as she wished to deny the possibility of their having created a child so quickly, the idea did not feel as repugnant as she originally thought it might be. The possibility of their sharing such great joy together pleased her. "You can no longer wait for the past to find you," she chastised, "when your future is on the other side of that door."

Rising, she crossed the room quickly, not stopping until

she had boldly opened the door on the other side of their shared sitting room to enter Darcy's bedchamber.

Barechested to the waist, her husband turned quickly to face her. "Elizabeth, are you well? Is something amiss?" he asked in concern. "Do you require my assistance?"

Her gaze slid to his bed and quickly back to his face. "I...I was...was thinking of...of our future."

A bit of hope crossed his features, but he did not move. "Do you wish to sleep in my bed this evening, instead of yours?"

Panic rushed to her chest, making it hard to breathe. "I wish—" she croaked.

He edged closer. "What do you wish, love?" he coaxed.

Elizabeth swallowed her fears. "I wish I could remember how it was between us. When you made me your wife."

He extended his hand to her. "You wish us to reclaim the magic we knew in Bath? The magic of us?"

Elizabeth took a half step forward, but did not reach for his hand. "Permit me to remind you I am as I was the first night we were together." She swallowed hard again. "I am in desperate need of the memory of us—of those nights when we were together. I require a new memory of us to replace the old ones."

She held her breath as she crossed the room to stand before the bed. Recapturing his gaze, which had turned hot in anticipation, she slid her arms from the satin wrapper and let it drop to the floor.

His breathing hitched higher. "Dearest God," he rasped. "Do not permit me to be dreaming." He paused so long Elizabeth began to feel awkward. At last, he hissed, "If you do not want this, say so now, for once I touch you, no honor exists that will compel me to stop."

"I want to be your wife in all ways," she insisted.

Evidently, her husband required no other encouragement. He scooped her into his arms to place her down gently upon his bed, following her down, to brace his weight above her. "Permit me to show you how it felt when we declared our love to the world."

Chapter 14

ELIZABETH AWOKE AND ROLLED over in Darcy's bed to discover him already up. She gathered his pillow and crushed it to her, deeply inhaling his scent—sandalwood and masculinity.

"You awake?"

She reached for the bed drape to tug it aside. "I thought you deserted me," she teased.

Her husband grinned at her. "Never in our lifetime could I leave you, love. I simply ordered Sheffield to fetch my lovely wife her morning tea and toast. I planned to rejoin you in our bed. I know you cannot survive a Derbyshire winter without my closeness."

"Think yourself indispensable, do you?" she taunted.

He walked casually toward the bed, peeling off his banyan as he went. Elizabeth's eyes grew wide, and she felt a blush rush to her cheeks, but she did not look away because Mr. Darcy standing before her as God had created him was a magnificent sight to behold.

"I am as you have made me, Elizabeth."

She opened her arms and her heart to him then. "Come. We have not much time. We cannot leave Georgiana alone to tend to the tenants when they call today."

Her husband ran a line of kisses across her shoulder blade. He murmured, "Mrs. Reynolds can assist my sister."

"Then everyone will think your wife is some sort of

monster you mean to hide away," she argued. "I can just see the story of a Gothic novel where a man attempts to hide away his Bedlam-bound wife in the attic of his manor house. Is that how you wish the gossips to talk about me?" she argued. Her fingers traced the curls at the nape of his neck.

"I know you speak in reason," he whispered close to her ear. "But all I wish is to remain with you, like this, until eternity. The only thing to make this more complete would be the return of your memories."

"The memories cannot be forced," she protested, attempting not to pull away from him, for the mention of her failures always placed a wall between them—a wall she wished to knock down with one swift and sure punch of her fist.

Noticing her reluctance, her husband pulled back. For an elongated moment, he stared at her and she at him. At length, he said, "I recognize how fragile your condition is." He sighed heavily. "I do not mean to sound as if I am a one-note musician, but despite the wonderful gift of the love you presented me last evening, I remain a selfish man. I understand your love for your parents, your sisters, your friends, our family, and, with God's grace, some day our children; yet, I require the special love shared by two people. A partner in life."

"And you do not believe I can be that type of woman?" she questioned. She rolled from his embrace.

He sat up in the bed. "How do I explain this without making you think poorly of me?" He paused as if to gather his thoughts. "If my body were made up of one hundred strands of devotion to our path to the future, ninety-nine would report for duty and never question our journey."

"But one part still questions whether I am practicing some sort of scheme," she accused.

"It is not that I any longer question your memory loss. In the beginning, I admit, I feared your disloyalty. I have suffered greatly, over the years, with Mr. Wickham's various betrayals, especially those that marred my father's memory and my sister's innocence. To have my wife call out his name while she remained

In Want of a Wife

in a most fragile state—to call for *Wickham*, rather than for me, still haunts me."

She closed her eyes as a numbness gripped her breath. "I wish I could change what occurred."

"I do not blame you." He reached for her and drew her back into his arms as he lay back against the pillows. She settled her head upon his chest, and Darcy stroked her arm. "Perhaps I should tell you of what I know of Mr. Wickham's activities since your accident."

"Have you encountered him?" she asked, raising her head to look down upon him. "I swear my only image of the man is from the miniature your father kept of him."

"He was on the street outside of Darcy House on the day of your accident. I did not see him at first, but Jasper and Mr. Farrin spotted him."

"Could I have also seen him?" she questioned. "Based on what you told me of his character in your letter, I cannot think I would forgive him for his perfidy."

"In truth, I know of no means for you to have seen him. Mr. Farrin says Wickham was beyond Darcy House, near the corner. If Farrin and Jasper had not been atop of the coach, they might not have spotted him. I was lifting you from the coach when you broke away from me. You called Wickham's name and raced away from me. It was only then that I caught a glimpse of him—when I chased after you."

"Perhaps I spotted him on the street as our carriage entered the square. I cannot say with certainty, but I do know I must have had a reason to chase after him—something beyond a desire for the man," she insisted. "After the accident, I lost all memory of why I ran in his direction, but, at the time of my chase, by all accounts, all I felt for him was disgust. If I saw him and gave chase, there must have been another reason. Do you know why Mr. Wickham was in London? Would Lydia have been with him? From what my father and Jane said of my younger sister, if Lydia was in London, she would wish to view Darcy House."

Darcy admitted, "There was a woman with him, but it was

not Mrs. Wickham. She called at Darcy House and asked for you, but Mr. Thacker told her you had yet to arrive, but were expected on that day."

Elizabeth scowled in concentration. "From what I know of Lydia, she would have demanded that Mr. Thacker bring tea and cakes while she waited." Consternation marked her brows. "The Wickhams have been married but four months. How dare Mr. Wickham desert Lydia? She is but sixteen and in a strange city."

"I have men checking on her to make certain her quarters are secure and she has food," he explained. "And I have contacted Father Bennet about the possibility of Mrs. Wickham returning to Longbourn."

"How long has Lydia been alone in Newcastle?" she demanded to know.

"Before we arrived in London, Wickham told his commanding officer of an uncle on his death bed, but Wickham has no uncle. He was to be absent from Northumberland for two weeks, but he remained from his duties for more than a month."

"Lydia must be very resourceful," she remarked, deep in thought. "More resourceful than most, but I should not be so surprised after hearing father's accounting of my sister's planned elopement."

"It is my understanding Captain Sullivan's wife has befriended your sister," he shared.

"That is good to know."

"Mrs. Bingley and your father sent Mrs. Wickham additional funds before I learned of Mr. Wickham's scheme to miss his duty," he shared.

She looked upon him in bewilderment. "You would protect Lydia despite her marriage to a man who has deceived you time and time again?"

"I arranged the marriage to protect Miss Lydia, but, more so, to protect you and your sisters. The tears in your eyes when you told me of her elopement was my impetus. If I could have convinced her to return to Longbourn with me, I would have done so, and your father could have married her off to someone more deserving, but Miss Lydia had set her heart on a man in uniform. Her plans to marry before any of her sisters outweighed any reasons I could provide her for the foolishness of her choices. Once everything was settled between Mr. Wickham and your sister and with Georgiana's encouragement, I renewed my proposal. Even then, I feared you could not understand how dearly I love you, and you would attempt to protect me with another refusal."

Her brows pulled together. "If Mr. Wickham was not with a dying uncle or his wife, what did he do with himself for a month?" She tapped his chest with her finger to emphasize her words. "I may not know our history, but I know your heart. If you thought I was in danger, you would make it your business to learn of Mr. Wickham's whereabouts. So, tell me what you know."

"Guilty, as described." A wry smile twisted his lips. "From what I learned from the men I employed to locate Mr. Wickham, he spent his time in London with a woman we originally identified as Mrs. Younge, Georgiana's former companion, the one who assisted him with his seduction of my sister, but Mr. Cowan erred. The lady was at a hotel in London, and, as you likely suspect, we assume she is the one who called upon Darcy House. Her description is too general for us to know her identity, and she, later, booked passage under an assumed name." He sighed heavily. "Later, Mr. Wickham traveled to Oxford for more gaming and a—"

"And a different woman," she finished for him.

"Yes, a different woman. One quite well known in the area. From there, he traveled the mail routes to Manchester."

"Such was your reason for leaving me alone at Pemberley?" she accused.

"I am sorry to have misled you, but, in light of your accident and what occurred during your recovery, it was important for me to confront him," he insisted.

"And did you confront him?" she demanded.

"We talked," he admitted, "but I could not ask him of his

interest in you. I could not ask of why he was in London just as we arrived at Darcy House."

"Because you feared his answer?"

"Because I knew I could not live without you, and if there was the smallest chance you meant to leave me, I did not want to know. It was better to remain in my ignorance."

※

Although he had objected quite adamantly, after breakfast, his wife had insisted that he inform Georgiana of Wickham's recent activities. "Your sister is stronger than you give her credit," Elizabeth had argued. "How can she think to ward off gentlemen with nefarious intentions if Georgiana knows nothing of the possibilities that a fine countenance can hide a heart reeking of evil? Do you wish her innocence to be a weight about her neck, as Wickham will prove to be the one about Lydia's neck for the remainder of her days?"

At length, her husband had done as she had asked, trusting his heart and his sister's growing maturity into her hands. Elizabeth was honored by his giving nature, for such meant they held a chance to know great happiness.

Elizabeth noted how Darcy had skimmed over the fact that Mr. Wickham had shared his bed with at least two other women since his marriage to Lydia, but the information had found a resting place upon Georgiana's conscience, for when the girl and Elizabeth spent time together later, Miss Darcy shared her concern.

"I could never be as forgiving of Mr. Wickham's dalliances as is your sister," she admitted. "Nor could I be so capable as to survive in a strange city without friends or connections. Mrs. Wickham must be quite remarkable."

"Naturally, I cannot claim actual knowledge of Lydia's nature, but, from Mrs. Bingley, I understand Lydia is quite adventurous. She takes each new experience as a challenge. I admit, I do wish Mr. Wickham was not so quick to abandon her for another. From what Jane says, Lydia fashions herself in love with Mr. Wickham."

"I understand perfectly," Miss Darcy whispered. "My heart thought itself engaged to the man."

"He fooled me also with his lies about your brother," Elizabeth confided. Although she recalled nothing of Mr. Wickham's actual nature, she knew, from Darcy's letter, of the lieutenant lying about a promise of a living and of the man's attempt to seduce Georgiana. Knowledge of either was enough for her to set the fellow aside. She simply wished she had confided something of the man's nature to her sisters before Lydia set her heart on the ill-begotten marriage.

"I do not imagine many women are immune to Mr. Wickham's charms." Georgiana mulled the idea over several times before adding, "Even this Mrs. Rosewood. I wonder who she could be. I can think of no one in the area with that name."

Later still, Elizabeth spent time in the library, not reading, but rather reliving both earlier conversations with Darcy. Viewing him with his customary guard brought low engendered emotions she could never have imagined. The simple remembrance of his weary countenance had her stomach lurching and her eyes tearing up in sympathy. She had been granted a rare opportunity to view him in a moment of impuissance. She doubted more than a few individuals knew him so well as she. Obviously, he had never permitted even his sister to know the depth of his struggles.

Elizabeth could not say when it had happened or even how, but within weeks of waking in an unfamiliar room with a stranger, she had fallen violently in love, for the second time, with the same man, just as Mr. Darcy spoke of his father falling repeatedly in love with Lady Anne. Her hand involuntarily came to rest upon where she suspected their child grew. She had the answer on how to make him happy. She would do whatever she must, for her husband deserved a wife who adored him.

Elizabeth awoke with a jolt. Awareness stormed her heart. She reached for Darcy, but he was not in the bed they shared. "The tenants' court," she murmured. Darcy had decided to reinstate his father's traditional "tenants' court," held on the last day of the year, where her husband would entertain grievances between cottagers and conduct other such business, beginning the new year, on the morrow, with an absence of previous restraints, gripes, or commitments. "But I must speak to him," she grumbled, tossing the bed linens aside and giving the bell cord a tug. "This cannot wait."

Hannah appeared before Elizabeth could begin to undress. "Permit me, ma'am," the maid said when she viewed Elizabeth's failed attempts to untie the laces holding her gown closed.

Elizabeth ignored the woman's fussiness. "I require a warm gown, and I must see Mr. Darcy at once."

"Yes, ma'am." Hannah selected a brown wool gown and wool stockings, as Elizabeth continued to undress. Within minutes, Elizabeth was clad in a proper gown. "Your hair, ma'am."

"It will wait, Hannah. I must find Mr. Darcy. I have remembered what happened with the letter and the carriage accident. I must find my husband and tell him. This is important. He must be made known to what occurred."

"The news of your memory is a blessing indeed, ma'am," the maid beamed with happiness. "But you cannot think to go out alone, ma'am. I will go with you."

Already gathering her scarf and gloves, Elizabeth ordered, "Then fetch your shawl and your cloak, Hannah."

Ten minutes later, Elizabeth exited Pemberley through a side door off the back parlor. Mr. Nathan had not approved of her going out so early. "It is bitterly cold, ma'am," he argued, but settled when she told him Hannah would accompany her.

"The tenants' court is being held at Brine Cottage," Hannah explained as they crossed the open lawn. The crunch of the frozen earth was the only sound she heard, for Elizabeth was intent on the dream. Tears filled her eyes, likely from the intense cold, but she could not know for certain if they were not instead from a mix of worry and relief.

"How far?" she managed to ask.

"A bit less than a mile," Hannah grunted. She caught

Elizabeth's arm and assisted her over an icy patch.

"I apologize for bringing you out on such a cold morning," she said lamely.

Hannah paused. "It be well, ma'am," she assured. "Days at Pemberley be more content since Mr. Darcy married you. Me and all the others at Pemberley are most obliged to serve you as we can, and if your memory has returned, then all the master's prayers have been answered. I wish to be witness to his relief."

Elizabeth laughed lightly. "I am glad to hear it, and you shall be happy to know Mr. Darcy's days will be easier after my visit with him this morning. After I tell him of the return of my memory, I mean to speak of the possibility of a child in the summer."

Hannah shot her a knowing look. Despite her promise to do otherwise, Elizabeth suspected Hannah had shared hints of a possible heir for Pemberley among those below stairs. Now that she thought back on it, a foot stool and an extra service of tea had become the norm of late. The fact she could be enceinte was another secret she no longer wished to hide from Darcy. They should step into the new year, hand-in-hand, and excited for what their days together would hold.

Settled in her resolve, Elizabeth picked her way along the path Hannah had indicated, enjoying both the exercise and the anticipation of sharing her revelations with Darcy.

Some ten minutes later, Hannah remarked with a pronounced shiver, "Not much further, ma'am. Less than a quarter mile. Just up around that stand of trees."

It was then Elizabeth noted the figure further along the path. The intruder's back was all she could view, but she knew the person's identity immediately. Silently, she signaled Hannah to step off the path. "Is there another means to reach the cottage?" she whispered close to Hannah's ear while motioning to the figure intent upon studying the road ahead.

With concern marking her features, Hannah nodded in the affirmative.

"Good," Elizabeth continued softly. "Fetch Mr. Darcy,"

she instructed. "Tell him Mrs. Rosewood awaits him along the path."

"But that be—" Hannah protested.

"I know," Elizabeth said calmly. "Just do as I ask. Mr. Darcy will understand. Now hurry, Hannah. Tell my husband, I shall require his assistance in this matter."

Chapter 15

DARCY SIMPLY WISHED TO return to his wife's bed and forget all this inanity between men who should know better. He was infinitely sorry he had agreed to reinstate the tenants' court this year. He should have permitted his steward to address disputes over sheep and water rights and, of all craziness, a broken window. With great difficulty, he stifled the sigh of exasperation rushing to his lips.

Unable to tolerate the feuding tenants one minute longer, he tapped sharply on the desk with his knuckles to earn their attention, while raising his voice to declare, "Enough!" He took a deep steadying breath before saying, "Mr. Stanley, I, most assuredly, do not pay you enough if this is the lunacy with which you must regularly deal." He noted Stanley ducked his head in amusement. "Although I have listened to your complaints for nearly ten minutes—six hundred precious seconds away from my family and you away from yours—I cannot find one morsel of sensibility in this feud." He pointed his finger at the first of the complainants. "Spindler, you did not see McConnel's son break your window; yet, you insist upon McConnel paying for the replacement."

"Maude Reynolds—" Spindler began, but Darcy silenced the man with his glare.

"This is my ruling: Mr. Spindler will make a public apology to Mr. McConnel on Friday, a week from tomorrow, at

Mr. Lambert's tavern. Two rounds of drinks will be placed on my account for all those in attendance to witness this apology. If that is done, I will pay for the window. If not, Spindler will pay for it himself." He pointed his finger at Spindler. "And note this, Mr. Spindler, long ago my father made stipulations for the maintenance of all the cottages upon Pemberley land. Part of those stipulations were for adequate light and ventilation for each. My father understood the diseases that could quickly claim a cottage's residents and even the possibility of illness spreading to all of the cottages without both. Placing wood in the opening will not satisfy those stipulations. Am I understood?"

Spindler ducked his head in subservience. "Yes, Mr. Darcy."

Darcy softened his tone. "Spindler, you must realize sometimes a man can stand for something so hard and so long that he does not realize he is actually sitting. Being too proud to extend one's hand to a neighbor breeds sad sorrows." Before Darcy could say more, a ruckus in the hallway had him rushing from the room.

"I tell you, I must speak to Mr. Darcy this second," Hannah screeched as one of the tenants attempted to shove her to the end of the line.

"What is it, Hannah?" he demanded as he approached the fracas. His tenants silenced. "Has something happened to Mrs. Darcy?"

Hannah glared at the man who had treated her so roughly. Darcy had no doubt the poor fellow would know the maid's wrath as soon as Darcy stepped from view. "Mrs. Darcy sent me to fetch you, sir."

Darcy caught Hannah's arm and pulled her into an empty room. "Tell me quick," he demanded in hushed tones. "Is Elizabeth unwell?" He did not dare to ask if she had waited until he left the house and had snuck out herself. He cursed himself for not letting go of his jealousy.

"Mrs. Darcy be on her way here. Your lady has remembered what occurred in London," Hannah said on a rush. "But before we arrived, Mrs. Darcy spotted a woman on the path leading to Brine Cottage. Mrs. Darcy be referring to the lady as a *Mrs. Rosewood*, but it really be Mrs. Avendell."

Elizabeth waited quietly for several minutes to permit Hannah time to make a circuitous path toward the cottage. She knew when Hannah came into view because Mrs. Avendell rose up on her toes for a better look at the path ahead. It was then she made herself known to the woman.

"If you are watching for my husband, Mrs. Avendell, I imagine you will be quite frozen through by the time he makes an appearance. I understand the tenants' court can last for hours. Perhaps you should simply take a place in line with the others to present your complaint."

The woman turned slowly to face Elizabeth. "I wondered when you would finally acknowledge me," the lady pronounced in cold tones.

"Perhaps my lack of response has more to do with your being forgettable than your charges against my husband. You really should not consider yourself a significant figure in either Mr. Darcy's life or mine," Elizabeth said as she squared her stance to make herself appear more formidable. Mrs. Avendell was further along the path that led gradually uphill, giving her the appearance of dominance, and Elizabeth meant to take away that advantage.

"You think I do not recognize the game you play? Mr. Darcy was to be mine, and then you waltzed yourself into his life. A damsel requiring a knight to save her. You think I do not know of your sister's planned elopement, and how Mr. Darcy forced his brother to marry your youngest sister."

"Mr. Darcy's brother?" Elizabeth snapped, with a laugh to mark the foolishness of the woman's words. "You think Mr. Wickham is my husband's brother? You have lived in this area most, if not all, of your life. When did you ever hear anyone of merit whisper words of scandal against the late Mr. Darcy? Is this nonsense what Mr. Wickham told you as part of his seduction?

With me, he spoke of a lost promise of the living at Kympton, but I quickly realized Mr. Darcy has too much honor to go against his father's wishes. Can you imagine one such as Mr. Wickham as a cleric? The poor parish would suffer from his lies and his hand in the tithe plate." She added another soft laugh to stall, hoping Mr. Darcy would soon make his appearance. "My brother-in-marriage is renowned for his creative falsehoods."

"You are confused, Mrs. Darcy." Mrs. Avendell said as she opened her cloak and caressed her growing midsection, which appeared significantly larger than the last time Elizabeth saw it. "It was not Mr. Wickham who seduced me, but rather your husband."

"The devil you say."

Elizabeth looked up to find a disheveled and scowling Darcy upon the path above where Mrs. Avendell stood.

"I believe I would recall if I chose to lie down with the likes of you, madam," her husband hissed.

"Then you remember our delightful rendezvous last July on this very path," Mrs. Avendell said sweetly.

Elizabeth knew her husband had had some sort of encounter with the woman, for she noted how his jawline tightened, but she had long ago taken Mr. Darcy's measure and knew, firsthand, something of his integrity. "My husband possesses too much honor to take advantage of any woman," she declared boldly. She paused before adding, "Even one who lurks in the woods of Pemberley, hoping to catch a glimpse of him. It was you on the main road the day I stopped for prayer, was it not?"

"You were so pitiful," Mrs. Avendell laughed. "Running away because I would not show myself as you had ordered me to do." The woman turned to Darcy. "Is this the type of woman you want as the mistress of Pemberley?" Mrs. Avendell pointed an accusing finger at Elizabeth. "A woman frightened by her own demons?"

Elizabeth shot a glance to her husband. He smiled upon her with the same look of satisfaction as she recalled from her dream. "If there are demons about, they sit upon your shoulders, madam." He spoke in his best Master of Pemberley voice, which softened when he looked again upon her. "Since I first set eyes upon my incomparable wife, I could never consider anyone else her equal, let alone her superior."

Elizabeth smiled brightly. "I am tolerable enough to tempt the man."

"You remember?" he asked in reverence.

"I remember it all," she assured him. "Netherfield and Rosings and Longbourn."

"Bless God," he responded solemnly.

Mrs. Avendell scowled before moving where she could block Elizabeth's view of Darcy. "Despite Mrs. Darcy's *infinite charms*, it is I who carries Pemberley's heir."

Darcy shoved past the woman to stand between her and Mrs. Avendell. "Although I had drowned my woes with more brandy than I should have consumed that late July day, all we have ever shared was the occasional 'good day' at your husband's establishment and three kisses upon this very path." He glanced over his shoulder at Elizabeth. "I beg your forgiveness, love. It was a rare moment of weakness, for which I have repeatedly experienced great shame."

"You sought the admiration of someone who would appreciate your *finer qualities*, am I not correct?" she asked in sympathetic tones.

"I did," he admitted. "But I erred greatly. I could not settle for someone strikingly inferior to the one woman who had claimed my heart, Miss Elizabeth Bennet of Longbourn."

"I would expect nothing less," Elizabeth declared boldly. She snuck a peek at Mrs. Avendell's expression of disapproval. "I should explain, sir, before you made yourself known to us, Mrs. Avendell was telling me how Mr. Wickham is your brother." Her husband's eyebrow hitched higher in obvious objection. "I suppose I should say half-brother to be more exact. She did not realize when Wickham refers to himself as being your 'brother,' he means his recent marriage to my sister, making the lieutenant a 'brother' in marriage only, not one with whom you share blood."

"Interesting. Especially as Mr. Wickham, who is my senior by some nine months, was born upon the Continent. He was alive for some two years before my late father employed Martin Wickham. The former Mrs. Wickham deserted her husband and son when George Wickham was but five. She was French, you see, and always considered herself unwelcomed by my parents and those in Derbyshire, especially those who had served with the late Mr. Wickham during the Fourth Anglo-Dutch War." He glared at Mrs. Avendell. "You may ask Lambton's mayor for confirmation of what I say. Mr. Saxby was Martin Wickham's commanding officer. Saxby recommended Martin Wickham to my father for the position of steward. The late Mr. Wickham was originally from Lincolnshire and had no connections to Derbyshire before arriving on Pemberley's threshold."

"You are mistaken," Mrs. Avendell charged.

Her husband's voice lowered in a menacing way. He ignored the woman's posturing. "After you have spoken to Mr. Saxby, I will expect you to issue me an apology for slandering my late father's good name with a tale of George Darcy's seduction of Christine Wickham. If not, I will personally make your life miserable."

Elizabeth also ignored the alarm crossing the woman's expression. It was important to make Darcy aware of all she now knew of Mrs. Avendell. "Before we departed Longbourn, in fact, before we were married, I received a letter from a *Mrs. Rosewood*, informing me that she was your mistress and was carrying your child."

Her husband's glare returned to Mrs. Avendell, but he still spoke to Elizabeth. "And?"

"The letter asked me to convince you to provide five thousand pounds to the letter's author and the child, or face the pain of your public unveiling as a debaucher of women," she explained.

"Why did you not confide in me?" he demanded.

"You had already spent more than my family could

afford to arrange Lydia's wedding," she said simply. "I had a conversation with myself and decided, if the letter was not another feeble attempt by Miss Bingley to have me call off the wedding, I could forgive you any former indiscretions. We would deal with the scandal if it came. You were sacrificing much to marry a woman with few connections to recommend her; the least I could do would be stand by your side and stare down any naysayers."

"I knew you to be surprisingly uncommon, Mrs. Darcy, but even I could not have imagined how singular God made you," he announced in loving tones.

Elizabeth nodded to Mrs. Avendell. "The lady sent me a second demand. It caught up with me in Bath."

"I see," he said ominously.

"I recently dreamed bits of what occurred," she admitted.

"I wish you had spoken of the dream before now," he said evenly.

"When the first dream came, you were in Manchester, and I could not make sense of whether the events actually happened or not." She shrugged in embarrassment. "I was furious when I received a second letter asking for five thousand pounds. I again burned the letter before you could see it. Attempting to make sense of the matter, I eliminated the letter you presented me at Rosings. I knew the incident was recent. Although, in my dream, I could not read the letter's contents, I wore the purple gown."

"The one Mrs. Gardiner insisted upon being a part of your trousseau?" he inquired.

Elizabeth said quietly. "It was only this morning that I managed to discover that *Mrs. Rosewood* and *Mrs. Avendell* were one and the same."

Realization formed in Darcy's eyes. "*Aven*, meaning a mountain wildflower of the rose family, and *dell*, a wooded valley. Very astute, my love."

"Mr. Wickham was on the street close to the park outside of Darcy House when you set me down. I had burned Mrs. Avendell's second letter right before we departed for London. It was only when I realized my sister's husband was in the City that

I suspected he had something to do with the letters. I chased after him to prevent his escape. I did not have time to explain."

Her husband reached out his hand for her. "I am grieved I ever doubted you."

However, before she could accept his hand, Mrs. Avendell's voice broke the spell between them. "Step from the way, Mr. Darcy."

Elizabeth swallowed her gasp. Mrs. Avendell held a Queen Anne pistol, and it was pointed at her.

"Put the gun away," Darcy ordered. He stepped between her and the woman, meaning to protect Elizabeth. "You cannot think I would look kindly upon anyone who meant to bring my wife harm."

"What do I care, if I cannot claim your affections? Why did you never notice me? At the assemblies? After Avendell's passing? All the others—"

"My father would never have permitted my doing so," Darcy reluctantly admitted, but Elizabeth realized, even if George Darcy had not objected to his son's pursuit of a girl who possessed the now Mrs. Avendell's forwardness, William would have been too shy to approach a girl with so open a nature.

"I was not good enough for your family," she charged. "I was not a gentleman's daughter. Is that it?"

"If I had loved you," her husband argued, "my father would have accepted my choice, but, in the days of our youth, my life was taken up with my university studies and all there was to learn of the running of Pemberley. I did not pursue any young girl in those days, barely permitting myself an evening out with friends. I did not know it then, but my father was very ill and dying. He forced himself to stay alive until I was in a position to run Pemberley on my own. There was no time for me to consider a relationship with anyone beyond my immediate family and estate counselors. As you said earlier, you were never without the attention of others."

"I never desired Avendell's attentions," she declared in bitter tones.

While Darcy argued with Mrs. Avendell, Elizabeth thought to step back out of Mrs. Avendell's range, but it was then she noticed a shadow form on the right side of the road. It took her a few brief seconds to realize the shadow was Hannah. Swallowing her fear for Darcy, she challenged the woman, "And so you think shooting me or Mr. Darcy will make it easier to convince my husband you are a better choice than I." It was important to convey the situation to Hannah.

A second shadow formed on the left, and Elizabeth allowed herself a breath before Mrs. Avendell drew her shoulders straight and lifted her arm to take aim, just as Hannah hefted a large rock from the ground and hurled it at Mrs. Avendell and Mr. Stanley charged at the woman.

As if in slow motion, the rock hit the woman in the side of her head throwing off her aim, and Darcy dove sideways, taking Elizabeth to the ground with him. The sound of the gunfire and the whistling of the bullet slid over their heads before she and her husband slammed hard into the frozen ground.

Behind them, Mrs. Avendell's protests filled the air, until a sharp slap brought an end to the woman's caterwauling.

Elizabeth caught a full breath, having her prior efforts driven from her lungs by the weight of William's body slamming into hers.

In a second, he was on his knees beside her. "Tell me you are well," he pleaded. Darcy's hands searched her body for any injuries, but she simply sighed with contentment. Her husband was safe, and she knew his protection and his love.

Elizabeth reached up to trace his jawline with her gloved fingers. "I imagine we will both be quite sore tomorrow, but I am unharmed." She caught his hand and placed it upon her midsection. "As is our child."

"Our...our child?" he stammered. "You...you are with child?"

"In case you have forgotten, we have been married eight weeks, and I have yet to have experienced my feminine flow." Surprisingly, a blush did not follow her declaration. This was

Darcy she was speaking to; there were no secrets between them.

"In truth, my mind was elsewhere. The possibility did not occur to me," he said, while wearing a silly grin.

She rose up on her elbows to give him a quick kiss. "Assist me up, Mr. Darcy," she ordered. "We will discuss how proud you must be of yourself once we reach Pemberley."

He laughed lightly. "We will spend tomorrow in bed, healing from this adventure *and enjoying my newly found possibilities.*" He stood and reached down for her.

Elizabeth rose gingerly. "That would be lovely," she grunted.

"Oh, goodness," he said as he knocked dirt from his breeches and her cloak. "I forgot. Tomorrow is the New Year. I am certain duties will fill my day."

Elizabeth caught his hand. "Listen to me, William. It shall all be well. Pemberley will not crumble into ruins in a day. You have said so yourself. Moreover, the first day of the year is the perfect time for us to place our family's needs before all others. Mrs. Bennet always said what one did on New Year's Day, he did all year round."

Darcy studied her for a few seconds before smiling. "I have been known to put great store in Mrs. Bennet's advice."

Elizabeth laughed. "Even when my mother called you a vain, disagreeable man?"

"Later, she termed me to be *charming* and *handsome*," he countered.

"Likely because you removed her most disagreeable daughter from Longbourn," Elizabeth said as she reached for his hand, more shaken than she realized.

He wrapped an arm about her to brace her against his side. "Permit me to see you home. I will send for a physician to examine you." He turned to his steward. "We must postpone the tenants' court until after Twelfth Night. I require you to see Mrs. Avendell into Lambton. I will ride into the village and lodge my complaint with the magistrate once I am certain Mrs. Darcy has not suffered from this incident."

Hannah pointed to a pile of rags at Mrs. Avendell's feet. "It appears in her struggle with Mr. Stanley, the village bookseller managed to lose her child. Her baby was no more than a pillow."

"I thought she had increased in girth dramatically since we saw her two weeks prior," Elizabeth declared as she hugged Hannah in appreciation. "I was never more glad to see you. How can I tell you how incredible you are and how blessed I am to claim you as my lady's maid, Hannah Tolliver? You are quite astounding, and I shan't forget this kindness. Ever."

"Neither will I," Darcy echoed Elizabeth's sentiments.

"I do not understand why Mrs. Avendell would permit others to think her carrying a bastard child when she was not enceinte. What type of woman welcomes the ruination of her reputation?" Darcy asked as they cuddled in bed after a hectic day of answering questions and postulating upon the bookseller's mental state.

"I suppose she thought your honor would compel you to act to protect her. Evidently, she dreamed of your completing the act you started upon the path." She attempted to remove all forms of chastisement from her tone, but she knew she had failed when he stiffened. Ignoring the obvious, she snuggled closer to him. "I fear I am sorer than I expected to be," she murmured against his chest.

As expected, her husband settled her gently upon the mattress before moving to a position where he might massage her legs as they spoke. "Even inebriated, I would remember if I had participated in a dalliance," he argued.

Elizabeth sighed with the pleasure of his touch. "Most assuredly, you would. I never thought to accuse you, only to reason out the unreasonable. Perhaps Mrs. Avendell planned to pretend the loss of the child after you married her, which would have been easier to do back in August. Hannah says the village speculated on our relationship, even then, especially after you brought Miss Darcy to meet me, and then you left the area shortly after I did. I frequented the bookstore when I stayed in Lambton;

Mrs. Avendell would have known there was a real possibility of her losing her chance to make you believe she carried your child. Desperation makes a sorry bedfellow. Her next opportunity to approach you about the child she carried would have been about the time you returned to Hertfordshire to bring Mr. Bingley back to Jane. You were gone from Pemberley from September to our recent return. She had started the tale and could not undo the rumors. By now, if she were carrying a child, she would have been five months along; thus, the pillow."

Darcy paused as if to consider her supposition before continuing to knead her legs' muscles. If she were truly pregnant, as she now hoped, his touch would be a welcomed addition to their nightly rituals, especially during her latter months. Her husband was quite skilled with his hands. He rolled her to her stomach to attend to her hips and back. She sighed her next question. "Do you suppose Mrs. Avendell was really with child at one time?"

"And transferred the deed to me?" he mused.

"It does seem odd," she reasoned. "There was all that talk of Mr. Wickham being your brother. Mayhap she thought if she could not have you, then a 'brother' was the next best thing. Is there any chance Mr. Wickham was in Derbyshire last July or perhaps the lady was in London? I know Wickham often carried messages to the Capital for Colonel Forster."

"That is a possibility. We know Mrs. Avendell was recently in London with Wickham. I can only suppose they meant to make contact with you there. They would have had no means of knowing you had burned the lady's letter."

"Could they have met to end the lady's pregnancy?" Elizabeth ventured.

Her husband stilled for a brief moment. "It would have been easier to do the deed in London than in Derbyshire where she is more well-known," Darcy considered.

"And between them, they concocted a scheme to claim more money from you," she surmised.

"I am at a loss as to what they planned," he admitted.

"Your supposition makes sense. All I do know is they remained in the Capital until we departed London. Wickham traveled toward Manchester; Mrs. Avendale toward Matlock. She made her mistake by having her late husband's family retrieve her from Matlock and return her to Lambton. With Mr. Cowan's men tracking 'Mrs. Rosewood' to Matlock, and her husband's nephew testifying to her travels, she will be held on charges of attempted murder and extortion."

"But why five thousand pounds?" Elizabeth asked with a gasp when her husband located a particularly sore spot on her backside. "I...I understand...the late Mr. Avendell was quite wealthy."

"And obviously unable to bring his wife to child," Darcy observed as he bent to lightly kiss the place beneath his hands. He sighed contentedly before continuing. "According to Saxby, who also serves as magistrate for the area, the store's account books show the business has decreased significantly since Mr. Avendell's death. He also shared news of numerous complaints against Mrs. Avendell's business practices delivered to his door. She forgets to order particular books for regular customers, and the lady has little knowledge of her stock and is unable to make recommendations when called upon to do so. I always knew her not to be the reader her husband was, but I did not realize the habit would manifest itself so critically. It seems her spending greatly outweighed her income."

"What of the shop? I would despise seeing Lambton lose its bookseller," she said as her husband's hands worked the soreness from her shoulders.

"The nephew I mentioned earlier is willing to assume the business. I have told Saxby I would stand the man a loan to restart the business."

Elizabeth rolled to her back and reached up to caress his cheek. "And what of Mr. Wickham?" she asked.

Her husband snorted his displeasure. "As usual, Wickham cannot be connected to any of this madness other than a possible bedding of the woman in London. With your sister forgiving him and his captain only assigning extra duties for his punishment, Wickham will simply know a bit of discomfort for what could have been another fleecing of my purse. I have no doubt once he had his hands on the money, he would have abandoned Mrs. Avendell and disappeared with their ill-gotten gains, leaving her stranded without a home or friends or her reputation. All Mr. Gardiner and I did in the business with your sister was to make Mr. Wickham solvent by paying his debts and purchasing his commission. Mr. Wickham has not the wealth or the status he has always coveted, and I doubt this will be the last time we must deal with him."

At length, too exhausted to continue their "what ifs," they settled in each other's arms. Firelight lit his bedchamber. Satisfaction rested between them, as he drew her closer. He cupped her face in his large hands and leaned down to kiss her. Elizabeth wrapped her arms about his neck.

Passionate silence followed for several minutes before he drew back to whisper, "Thank our Lord, you are safe." He feathered a kiss across her brow. Darcy closed his eyes as if to drive away the images of their earlier fright. "When I think of the pain I caused you—" He looked away in obvious grief.

"I should have shown you the letters. If I had, neither of us would have been surprised to view Mr. Wickham in London, and perhaps you would have also noted Mrs. Avendell's presence, and we would have resolved all this madness weeks earlier." She glanced hesitantly at him. "Do you think there will ever come a day when we do not misunderstand each other?"

He cupped her chin, using his thumb to stroke her bottom lip. "As long as you agree we can settle our differences in one of our beds, we will survive the future well."

Elizabeth looked upon him with a wealth of tenderness and love. She feathered a kiss across his mouth, but he chose to deepen it. "I love you, Fitzwilliam Darcy," she said on a rasp.

"And I love you, Elizabeth Darcy. You are the essence of all things right in this world, and your love fills my heart with joy."

Epilogue

LATE AUGUST, 1813

"DOES IT EVER BECOME easier, Father Bennet?" Darcy paused in his pacing to glance again to the hall, expecting any moment to receive word of Elizabeth. In the family wing, his wife was giving birth to their first child, and he despised not being permitted to be with her.

Her parents had arrived some three weeks earlier for Elizabeth's lying in. Darcy was certain Mrs. Bennet was equally happy to be visiting at Pemberley as she was to have first hand knowledge of the Bennets' first grandchild. But, as Elizabeth had expressed a desire to have her mother close for the delivery, Darcy had extended the invitation. Mr. Bennet had been equally pleased to claim residence in Darcy's library and to view for himself how well his favorite daughter had recovered from her recent trials.

"I cannot say, Darcy," Mr. Bennet responded with a shrug of his shoulders. "After Elizabeth, I quit counting."

"Will she survive this?" Darcy feared losing Elizabeth as much as he feared losing the child and what that tragedy would do to his wife. He despised exposing his shortcomings to anyone, but he surely wished his own father was with him at the moment to provide him much needed advice.

"My Elizabeth is stronger than any of my other daughters.

I will not countenance losing her again, and I have warned God not even to consider such a travesty. The world cannot survive without my Lizzy's goodness and her wit. The last time—when she forgot her quintessence—it nearly killed me. If it was not for the image of Collins at Longbourn, haunting my days, touching my things, my books, while the rest of my family suffered, I doubt I would have much cared if the Lord took umbrage with my rants. Now that Elizabeth is well-settled, I have set my mind to outliving Collins. Do you not think it appropriate that the ninny would spend the remainder of his days playing toady to your aunt?"

Ignoring the cut of his clothes, Darcy collapsed in a nearby chair. "Considering that my aunt's cleric once aspired to be Elizabeth's husband, I possess little sympathy for Mr. Collins. Live another fifty years, Father Bennet."

Mr. Bennet chuckled. "Excellent advice, my boy. If I deny Collins and his line—may he sire only daughters as I have— the estate will revert to the Scottish branch of the family. I am on good terms with the Flynns. Their estate in Scotland is smaller than Longbourn, but quite profitable. You would enjoy their company, Darcy. I hold no doubt they would do better by Longbourn than Collins ever will."

Darcy let the comment about someone other than Collins slide for now. His mind was really not on the conversation, other than as a means to pass the time, but rather on the room upstairs that held his wife. Distractedly, he said, "Even if Collins does sire a son, perhaps the lad will take after Mrs. Collins, rather than his pater. Other than her choice of husbands, I always found Mrs. Collins quite sensible, and, according to Elizabeth, the lady had few choices at her age, which is the same as mine."

"I suppose if Collins is eventually to know Longbourn, despite my prayers to the contrary, then I should amend my talks with God to include the hope of Charlotte Collins influencing her son, if for no other reason, than the tenants I will leave behind to Collins's care. They deserve better than Collins." He paused as if considering his choice of words. "I fear God thinks me too vain to tolerate my prayers for longevity, and that grieves me." He sighed heavily. "I have asked God to permit me to live longer than Mrs. Bennet: Francis blames herself for not producing an heir for Longbourn. If I outlive her, she will not witness the Collinses displacing her."

"Bingley and I will see Mrs. Bennet is well-situated," Darcy assured.

"I know you will. I never thought otherwise. However, I would like to spare my wife the degradation of being driven from her home. Losing Elizabeth's presence in my life, even though only for a few months, had me examining my ways. I should have learned my lesson after Lydia's marriage disaster, but I could not seem to break with my old manner of doing things. Then Elizabeth's accident occurred, and I never prayed as hard as I did during that time. As my daughter had to learn to trust again, so did I. Although I was slow to admit my shortcomings, I am ashamed to say I have sadly neglected my family. I mean to emulate you, Darcy. I originally thought to include Bingley in the recasting of my life, but Jane's husband is too easily persuaded. You, on the other hand, possess both a steady and a compassionate nature. You would never permit Elizabeth her way if you knew it would place her in danger."

Darcy studied the man, wondering what to say. He settled on: "I am honored by the trust you have placed in me."

Bennet winked at him. "Enough maudlin. I have great aspirations, but no one is warranting I will know success. For now, I expect you to leave a man to his book and his glass of brandy while you see my Lizzy to health. I am certain, by now, Mrs. Bennet's presence in the room is no longer welcomed by Elizabeth. They are of very different natures."

"The last time I attempted to enter my wife's chambers, I was sent away," Darcy argued.

Mr. Bennet chuckled again. "Surely you are of a sterner disposition than what you describe. I have witnessed you quieting a room with a hard glare. I assure you, the only one in Elizabeth's chambers who does not fear you is my daughter. I tell you, Elizabeth requires your presence to know calm. I guarantee, by this time she is questioning whether she can finish the deed. You must add your courage to hers. And if Mrs. Bennet objects, remind her I did the same for her with three of our daughters before she thought herself capable of delivering a child without my presence in the room."

Darcy required no other encouragement. Within a minute, he was outside his wife's door, hand raised to knock; however, a scream like none he had ever heard previously had him sending the door slamming back into the wall and his storming into the dark room. "Dearest Lord!" He looked about the room in bewilderment. "Are you attempting to roast my wife alive? What is this nonsense?" It was August, and there was a fire blazing in the hearth. He caught an ewer of water and threw it on the fire. Crossing to the windows, he pulled back the drapes to let in the light and opened the window. "This is not a medieval household!"

Turning toward the bed where his wife lay in a crumpled heap, his hands fisted at his side. If he could strike someone, he would. His Elizabeth was pale and hollow-eyed.

"Mr. Darcy —" Mrs. Bennet began her chastisement, but a flick of his wrist and a quick hiss of disapproval silenced his wife's mother.

He crossed to the bed and gathered Elizabeth to him. "I am here," he whispered.

"I cannot go on," she rasped.

"You can," he insisted. "My Elizabeth would never abandon our family." He prayed he was not providing her false hope. He did not know what to do to assist her.

"I can truly do no more," she argued.

"We are together," he assured her. "Nothing can defeat us when we are together."

"Her pain comes every five minutes," Mrs. Bennet said from somewhere behind him. "But, for more than an hour, it has not progressed further."

Darcy was not certain what that meant, but he assumed

from the anxiety buried in Mother Bennet's tone, such was not good tidings. "Then we must assist her. Fetch Elizabeth a fresh gown, Mother Bennet."

"Lizzy does not require a clean gown," Mrs. Bennet argued.

Darcy cut her off before she could continue—before she could pronounce Elizabeth's coming demise. His wife was already frightened, and he would not permit Elizabeth to consider any outcome other than her and the baby surviving. "Elizabeth will feel better if she has a clean gown." He lifted his wife from her bed to carry her into his chambers where the air was fresh and inviting. He paused only briefly. "Give the bell a tug, love. Summon Hannah to assist you," he said softly, before positioning his wife in his arms and to carry her forward. Reaching his suite, he rested Elizabeth upon his lap, against his chest, while he sat and caught his breath. *What am I to do?*

"William," she whispered against the lawn of his shirt, "what if?"

"I will never stop loving you, Elizabeth. Even if there are no children, my love for you will remain true."

She nodded weakly until another of the pains caught her. She stiffened in his arms, attempting to disguise it.

"Scream if you must," he encouraged. "I will hold you."

She opened her mouth and emitted the most painful scream he had ever heard. It was all he could do not to shove her away. However, he made himself tighten his hold on her instead.

"Here is Mrs. Darcy's gown, sir."

He looked up to see his wife's maid. "Hannah, I am glad you are here. Your mistress requires your care."

"Yes, sir."

He lifted Elizabeth from his lap to place her in the chair. "Remove her soiled gown and drape her in the clean one. Wipe her face and arms with a cool cloth. I will return in a moment."

"Yes, sir."

Darcy hurried from the room before his wife could lodge an objection, but he was stopped in the passageway by the midwife. "Mr. Darcy, I must protest."

"Your services are no longer required, Mrs. Borden," he barked as he shoved past her.

"You are taking responsibility if you dismiss me. Your wife's death will be on your hands."

Darcy paused on the stairs. "My wife will not die, for if she does, so shall Pemberley, for she is the heart and soul of this estate. Now remove yourself from my presence or I will personally throw you out onto the lawn.

Anger carrying him forward, he rushed to the library. "Father Bennet, Elizabeth needs you."

Without looking back, Darcy returned to his chambers. Mr. Bennet's steps following close behind.

"What is this?" Mr. Bennet asked as he rushed into the room and knelt before his daughter.

"I cannot do this." Elizabeth rested her head against her father's shoulder.

"Lizzy has not progressed past five minutes," Mrs. Bennet provided them her evaluation of the situation.

Mr. Bennet glanced to his wife. "As you did with Mary. Did you learn nothing that day?" He leaned Elizabeth's limp form back into the cushions of the chair. "We must have Elizabeth up and moving."

Darcy glanced to this wife. "In her condition? Do you think that wise? The room was so hot when I arrived, I am surprised they had not all melted away."

Mr. Bennet glared at his wife. "Francis, you know better."

"But Mr. Darcy hired the midwife," she protested. "I only acted as the woman prescribed."

"We will not argue blame now," Mr. Bennet declared in a no-nonsense voice that Darcy had rarely heard the man use. He turned to Darcy. "I will assist Elizabeth to her feet. Meanwhile, you must send for one of your tenants, your housekeeper, a servant, anyone who can assist us once this baby means to make his or her entrance into the world. My expertise in this matter does not go further than this."

Darcy did not wait for additional instructions. His wife's life was in his and her father's hands.

※

"He is perfect, Lizzy," Darcy whispered close to her ear.

"Bennet," she murmured, as her eyes drifted closed. "Do not forget his name."

"I have not forgotten, my love." He kissed her forehead. "Now, you are to rest. The world will not stop spinning while you recover. I love you, my Elizabeth."

Naturally, she did not hear him, but Darcy was not upset she had not responded. He carried his wife's miracle in his arms.

He and Mr. Bennet had, literally, taken turns walking Elizabeth up and down the long passage of the family quarters for what felt like hours, but only a little over one hour before her pain lost some of its severity. They permitted her a bit of weak tea and warm broth whenever she reached the end of the hall and before she made her return. Their purpose was to bring a bit of color back to her cheeks and give her the strength to carry on, while providing time for his staff to reset her bedchamber with fresh linens and a quick cleaning.

Even after her severe pains subsided, Mr. Bennet insisted on continuing their trek until Elizabeth's contractions were some three minutes apart. Then instead of returning her to his bed, they had led her into her chambers where Mrs. Reynolds had set up a contraption like nothing Darcy had ever seen before, but one his housekeeper had fetched down from the attic. "After her two miscarriages, Lady Anne had this birthing chair brought in for her delivery of Miss Darcy. It was ahead of its time then." She paused awkwardly before assuring, "Your mother swore it made the difference."

Meanwhile, Mrs. Cameron had arrived at Pemberley's door. At Hannah's suggestion, Darcy had sent for the lady. According to Hannah, those who could not afford Mrs. Borden's services often called upon Mrs. Cameron.

The woman had proven to be sensible and knowledgeable. With Mr. Bennet's exit, Darcy assisted Elizabeth to the chair and waited for Mrs. Cameron to order him from the room. Even though he had no intention of leaving his wife alone again. As one of his cottagers, he was not certain how she would react to his being in the birthing room. The woman, however, simply eyed him with amusement, before shrugging her acceptance. "You'll bathe Mrs. Darcy's brow and keep her calm. If she be requirin' somethin' to squeeze while reacting to the pain, you'll offer yer hand," she instructed.

"Yes, ma'am. In this matter, you are the master."

His words appeared to please Mrs. Cameron. Within another hour, she placed his son into his arms, while the woman and Mrs. Bennet saw to Elizabeth passing the birth sack.

While they saw to his wife's exhaustion and her comfort, Darcy had carried the boy downstairs and introduced him to the child's equally proud grandfather. "Thank you, Father Bennet," he said as he placed the boy in Mr. Bennet's waiting arms. "Without your good sense, my son might never have known his first breath."

Mr. Bennet's eyes teared up in tenderness. Without removing his eyes from the child, he asked, "And Lizzy?"

"Completely spent, but Mrs. Cameron declares she will heal quickly and be bossing us both around soon."

"Excellent," Mr. Bennet whispered. "I recall when they placed Elizabeth in my arms. Frances was so certain Elizabeth would be a boy and openly lamented her regrets, but I shushed my wife immediately, telling her I could not be happier, for, you see, Elizabeth's small fingers had latched onto mine. I had no care whether she was another daughter. Jane was always shy, but, from the beginning, Elizabeth claimed me as her favorite parent. She would sneak into my study and come and sit on my lap and tell me of her day. It took some time before I could understand her babbling, but that did not matter. I never knew such joy."

They sat in comfortable silence for several minutes, before Mr. Bennet said in reverent tones, "Both our prayers have been answered." He rose to hand the child back to Darcy. "I am not certain God will any longer entertain my request to outlive

Collins, especially after I filled his ears with my recent laments in Elizabeth's favor." Clearing the rasp from his throat, he declared, "I require a brandy."

Darcy watched as his father-in-marriage poured himself a drink and took a sip. Darcy placed the boy on his shoulder to rock him to sleep. "You should know," he said softly so as not to disturb the child, "before your arrival at Pemberley, Elizabeth and I agreed that if we were blessed with a son, we would name him, Bennet George Samuel Darcy."

Her father paused in reflection. "A bit of me will remain even after my days know an end. Thank you, Darcy."

"Fifty years, Father Bennet," Darcy said with a grin. "Elizabeth, my son, and I will be counting on your advice for, at least, another fifty years."

Mr. Bennet raised his glass in a salute. "Fifty years of watching my grandchildren spread the best of me out into the world, such a prospect will suit me just fine."

Finis

Other Novels by Regina Jeffers

Jane Austen-Inspired Novels:

Darcy's Passions: Pride and Prejudice Retold Through His Eyes
Darcy's Temptation: A Pride and Prejudice Sequel
Captain Frederick Wentworth's Persuasion: Jane Austen's Classic Retold Through His Eyes
Vampire Darcy's Desire: A Pride and Prejudice Paranormal Adventure
The Phantom of Pemberley: A Pride and Prejudice Mystery
Christmas at Pemberley: A Pride and Prejudice Holiday Sequel
The Disappearance of Georgiana Darcy: A Pride and Prejudice Mystery
The Mysterious Death of Mr. Darcy: A Pride and Prejudice Mystery
The Prosecution of Mr. Darcy's Cousin: A Pride and Prejudice Mystery
Mr. Darcy's Fault: A Pride and Prejudice Vagary
Mr. Darcy's Present: A Pride and Prejudice Holiday Vagary
Mr. Darcy's Bargain: A Pride and Prejudice Vagary
Mr. Darcy's Brides: A Pride and Prejudice Vagary
Elizabeth Bennet's Deception: A Pride and Prejudice Vagary
Elizabeth Bennet's Excellent Adventure: A Pride and Prejudice Vagary
The Pemberley Ball: A Pride and Prejudice Vagary
A Dance with Mr. Darcy: A Pride and Prejudice Vagary
The Road to Understanding: A Pride and Prejudice Vagary
Pride and Prejudice and a Shakespearean Scholar: A Pride and Prejudice Vagary
Where There's a FitzWILLiam Darcy, There's a Way: A Pride and Prejudice Vagary
In Want of a Wife: A Pride and Prejudice Vagary
Honor and Hope: A Contemporary Pride and Prejudice

Regency and Contemporary Romances:

The Scandal of Lady Eleanor, Book 1 of the Realm Series (aka A Touch of Scandal)
A Touch of Velvet, Book 2 of the Realm Series
A Touch of Cashémere, Book 3 of the Realm Series
A Touch of Grace, Book 4 of the Realm Series
A Touch of Mercy, Book 5 of the Realm Series
A Touch of Love, Book 6 of the Realm Series
A Touch of Honor, Book 7 of the Realm Series
A Touch of Emerald, The Conclusion of the Realm Series
His American Heartsong: A Companion Novel to the Realm Series
His Irish Eve
Angel Comes to the Devil's Keep, Book 1 of the "Twins" Trilogy
The Earl Claims His Comfort, Book 2 of the "Twins" Trilogy
Lady Joy and the Earl: A Christmas Novella
Letters from Home: A Christmas Novella
Beautified by Love
Christmas Ever After: A Clean Regency Romance Anthology
Second Chances: The Courtship Wars
One Minute Past Christmas, A Holiday Short Story

Coming Soon...

Lady Chandler's Sister, Book 3 of the "Twins" Trilogy

The Heartless Earl: A Common Elements Romance Project Novel

Indentured Love: A Persuasion Vagary

Obsession

Meet Regina Jeffers

Writing passionately comes easily to Regina Jeffers. A master teacher, for thirty-nine years, she passionately taught thousands of students English in the public schools of West Virginia, Ohio, and North Carolina. Yet, "teacher" does not define her as a person. Ask any of her students or her family, and they will tell you Regina is passionate about so many things: her son, her grandchildren, truth, children in need, our country's veterans, responsibility, the value of a good education, words, music, dance, the theater, pro football, classic movies, the BBC, track and field, books, books, and more books. Holding multiple degrees, Jeffers often serves as a Language Arts or Media Literacy consultant to school districts and has served on several state and national educational commissions.

Jeffers's writing career began when a former student challenged her to do what she so "righteously" told her class should be accomplished in writing. On a whim, she self-published her first book *Darcy's Passions*. "I never thought anything would happen with it. Then one day, a publishing company contacted me. They had watched the sales of the book on Amazon, and they offered to print it. The rest is history."

Since that time, Jeffers continues to write. "Writing is just my latest release of the creative side of my brain. I taught theater, even participated in professional and community-based productions when I was younger. I trained dance teams, flag lines, majorettes, and field commanders. My dancers were both state and national champions. I simply require time each day to let the possibilities flow. When I write, I write as I used to choreograph routines for my dance teams; I write the scenes in my head as if they are a movie. Usually, it plays there for several days being tweaked and *rewritten,* but, eventually, I put it to paper. From that point, things do not change much because I have completed several mental rewrites."

Every Woman Dreams

Regina Jeffers's Website

Austen Authors

Discover Regina on…

Facebook, Pinterest, Twitter, LinkedIn, Goodreads, and Amazon Author Central

Chapter 1

"Here come the lovers, full of joy and mirth. — Joy, gentle friends! Joy and fresh days of love accompany your hearts!"
William Shakespeare, *A Midsummer Night's Dream*, Act V, Scene i

2 December 1815

James Highcliffe, 10th Earl Hough, stepped into the crowded ballroom. He knew his appearance would cause a stir. He had never been one to frequent the entertainments, but Lady Jocelyn Lathrop had been pressed into service as her niece's sponsor to finish off the Season, and so James had agreed to aid her brother as escort to Lady Jocelyn and Lady Constance, for the last fortnight of the girl's Come Out.

James's motives were certainly not all charitable, for his curiosity regarding Lady Jocelyn had never waned. He had desired the former Lady Jocelyn Powell since he discovered girls were more than silly nuisances. Their families' estates marched along together on one side, and James had known Joy, as her family and friends called her, his whole life.

As if it were yesterday, he recalled the day he had first kissed her—a sloppy, too much mouth kiss that captured his heart immediately. After that momentous occasion, James had kissed her often, each time with more fervor. He also recalled how his father had pulled him into his study when news reached

Robert Highcliffe's ears that his only son had set his eyes on Lord Powell's daughter. It was not as if Jocelyn Powell would be a bad match socially, for his father was an earl, but hers was a marquess. On the contrary, the match would have been perfect except for the fact Robert Highcliffe, 9th Earl Hough, had contracted away James's future while James was still in the cradle.

"Your choice of a bride is not yours to make," his father had explained to a shocked James. "An agreement exists between our family and that of Lord Connick. You have been betrothed to Miss Louisa Connick since the girl's birth."

Naturally, James had argued over the fairness of such an arrangement, but earned no concessions on his father's part. In the end, he had sat in witness as Jocelyn—*his Joy*—married Lord Harrison Lathrop, a man James had never liked, but even more so for stealing Jocelyn away. Shortly after her departure from Yorkshire, James recited his vows with Louisa. Jocelyn removed to her husband's estate in Kent, while he and Louisa resided at Hough Hall, never again to travel in the same circles.

"Hough?" a very masculine voice called before James received a testing male slap on the back. "I thought Caroline spoke of the Second Coming of our Lord when she declared your presence in Lady Beauchamp's ballroom. Whatever has you making an appearance so late in the Season?" Lord Beeson asked. "Do not tell me you mean to do the pretty. Thinking of taking on one of this year's crop as your new countess?"

James had waited eighteen months after Louisa's passing to venture out into Society again. He wanted no gossip regarding his planned pursuit of Lady Lathrop. He and Louisa had spent twenty-two years together, but the last three, she had not left her bed for more than her personal needs. For two and twenty years, he had served his duty to the earldom. Now, he planned to serve his duty to his heart.

"I promise you, Beeson, I am too old to chase after a young skirt, not even half my age. I simply promised Lord Powell I would make certain his sister and daughter were safely escorted this evening and until the two return to Powell Manor

Excerpt from "Lady Joy and the Earl: A Regency Christmas Novella"

for Christmastide. His lordship was unexpectedly called home to Yorkshire. Lady Constance has agreed to perform at a musicale before her return, so Powell left her under his sister's care and my oversight."

"Now that you mention it, I recall your and Powell's estates align, do they not?" Beeson nodded his understanding.

"Yes, they do. We have been friends since childhood. We each came into our titles within a year." James's eyes scanned the ballroom, searching for Jocelyn. At last they found her. "If you will pardon me, Beeson, I should inform Lady Lathrop of my arrival."

Beeson chuckled. "I imagine Lady Lathrop is well aware of your presence in the ballroom. Every unattached female, as well as many attached ones, have turned their eyes in your direction."

Even before she turned around, Jocelyn knew Lord Hough had entered the ballroom. A hush fell over those in attendance, followed by a swell of whispers. Slowly, she pivoted to take in the magnificence of the man. James Highcliffe stood beneath the archway, his still muscular frame filling the opening. A tall figure dressed in black. Except for the blue hue of his waistcoat, he reminded her of a character from a Minerva Press romance. He was not as lean as she remembered, but there was nothing amiss with the manner in which his evening clothes set off his figure.

Irritably, she realized she held her breath until his gaze found hers. A slight smile lifted his lips. Their gaze held for several elongated ticks of the clock. Jocelyn could not look away. She knew she should turn and pretend not to notice his presence; yet, like a ninny, she studied his approach, enjoying the ease with which he moved. He was the one by whom she judged all other males — unfortunately, he was the one who had broken her young heart.

Jocelyn purposely turned to remind her niece Constance not to appear too eager to greet Lord Hough. "It would be unseemly," she whispered her caution.

"But it was kind of his lordship to agree to escort us, Aunt."

"It was," Joy reluctantly agreed. When she learned her brother had made arrangements with Lord Hough without consulting her, she was most upset at the prospect of encountering the earl again. She had been in Kent with Lathrop when James Highcliffe spoke his vows to another, and she was glad for it. Such was the reason she had agreed to an earlier date for her nuptials than the one James had named. Jocelyn knew she was not strong enough to witness his marrying another. "I forget you see Lord Hough often at home."

"More so since the death of his wife," Constance explained. "But often enough, at church and such. How long has it been since you encountered Lord Hough?"

"Twenty-two years, four months, and eighteen days," his lordship responded before Jocelyn could claim her wits about her.

Constance's mouth stood agape in astonishment. "How can you be so certain, my lord?"

Lord Hough winked at Constance before presenting Jocelyn's niece a proper bow, a reminder to Constance to respond accordingly. "I recall clearly, Lady Constance, for that was the day Lady Jocelyn married Lord Lathrop, and the viscount spirited away Aberford's sunshine."

Jocelyn willed the embarrassment from her cheeks. "Lord Hough bams you, Constance. His lordship possesses a great sense of humor." The fact the numbers he quoted were accurate to the day of her exchanging her vows with Harrison Lathrop not only surprised her, but irritated her. Lord Hough had walked away from their blossoming romance when he was nineteen and she several months on the other side of sixteen. Two years later, she became Lady Lathrop. Four months later, James married Lady Louisa Connick, a woman he had never courted. For more than two decades, except for one brief encounter after her father's death, they had never stood in the same room together, certainly never side-by-side.

Excerpt from "Lady Joy and the Earl: A Regency Christmas Novella"

Before Jocelyn could continue, Lord Sheldon appeared at Constance's side. "Lady Constance, I believe this is our dance. The set is forming."

"May I be excused, Aunt?"

"Certainly." Jocelyn deliberately nodded to Lord Sheldon. "I shall be waiting here for my niece's return."

"Yes, ma'am."

Attempting to ignore the very masculine man standing beside her, Jocelyn watched Constance as her niece and Sheldon took their places in the set.

"Would you care to dance, Joy?" Hough asked softly.

Despite her best efforts, Jocelyn's heart hitched higher just hearing her family's pet name for her on Lord Hough's lips.

In a frustrated warning to control her emotions, her eyebrows drew together in a fierce frown. "A chaperone does not dance," she chastised.

When she turned to him, his cinnamon-colored eyes presented her a long, slow look. Staring into those eyes, Jocelyn recognized the familiar merriment she had known years prior. "Do you not recall the steps, my lady?" he teased.

"When was the last time you danced, James Highcliffe?" she challenged.

"Your sixteenth birthday," he said without hesitation.

The idea shocked her. "Surely you and Lady Hough shared a dance upon occasion."

His brow climbed a fraction. "I am not accustomed to exaggerating when speaking of momentous events. I assure you, Louisa and I never danced. My late wife despised the exercise, but I recall your being quite fond of twirling about a dance floor, as well as your being excessively light on your feet and on mine."

Jocelyn blushed and covered the emotion with a flick of her fan. "Not any longer," she said tersely. "Girlish fantasies. A woman who has borne two sons can no longer be termed *light on her feet*."

Lord Hough leaned closer to whisper in her ear. "Do not fish for compliments, Joy, for you must surely own a looking

173

glass. But if you do not, simply know, in my eyes, you remain the most beautiful woman of my acquaintance."

"Your lordship—" She meant to caution him against such forwardness, but her eyes landed upon his lips, and all thoughts of anything but whether his kiss would be as exciting as the last one they had shared filled her brain.

"No reprimands," he said in what appeared to be bemusement, "or I will be compelled to kiss you into silence."

Joy struggled against the shiver of desire skittering up her spine. There was a time the man standing before her was her world. She would not make that mistake again. Lathrop had taught her all the lessons she required about disappointment.

"No kissing, my lord," she hissed through tight lips. "No cuddling. No dancing. No flirting. I am Constance's chaperone, and, until my brother's return, you are our escort. If you are interested in female companionship, I am certain there are many in this ballroom willing to oblige you, whether you desire a mistress or a wife."

His voice, when responding, was both low and demanding. "We will kiss, Lady Lathrop." His words were quiet and deliberately stressed. "And cuddle and flirt and dance. And when *I choose* a wife, it will be you. I will have no mistress—only you, Joy, as the chatelaine of my manor and of my life."

"Most assuredly, you jest. We have not laid eyes on each other for twenty years, and you expect me to consider marriage to a man I barely know."

"You know me, Joy. It was Lathrop you did not know." They stared at each other in unrelenting stubbornness. "If you require my services, my lady, I will be playing cards."

Jocelyn watched him walk away. She remained frozen to the spot. James Highcliffe wanted her as his wife. How absurd! Once, such had been her dearest dream, but fancy was no longer a part of her nature. Any whimsical bits of her character had been dutifully drummed from her by her late husband. "Less than a fortnight," she reminded herself. "Then Lord Hough will again be gone from my life. I shall return to Kent and my simple existence.

I prefer my days without all the chaos a husband brings. No more will I place my faith in another—in one who promises the world with one hand and snatches it away with the other."

Resolve settled in her shoulders: The temptation to kiss Lord Hough again as she once had done would not come about. Harrison Lathrop had not broken her. Neither would Lord Hough. "It will not happen," she whispered. "I am no longer the naïve girl his lordship once knew."

Made in the USA
Monee, IL
20 April 2021